SHOOTING GALLERY

"Kill him," Sparrow Hawk said.

Steel blades gleamed and lances were raised.

Fargo threw himself backward and clawed at the Colt. "I do not want to shoot you," he shouted.

They weren't listening. The warrior with the long nose stabbed at his leg, and missed. Lunging, the warrior raised his knife to bury it in Fargo's stomach. Fargo shot him. A lance dug into the ground next to his chest.

The man holding it hiked it to thrust again. Fargo shot him. Sparrow Hawk had an arrow nocked and was bringing it to his cheek to aim. Fargo shot him. A fourth warrior leaped, his eyes agleam with bloodlust, his knife poised to kill. . . .

THE
TRAILSMAN
#352

TEXAS
TANGLE

by

Jon Sharpe

A SIGNET BOOK

SIGNET
Published by New American Library, a division of
Penguin Group (USA) Inc., 375 Hudson Street,
New York, New York 10014, USA
Penguin Group (Canada), 90 Eglinton Avenue East, Suite 700, Toronto,
Ontario M4P 2Y3, Canada (a division of Pearson Penguin Canada Inc.)
Penguin Books Ltd., 80 Strand, London WC2R 0RL, England
Penguin Ireland, 25 St. Stephen's Green, Dublin 2,
Ireland (a division of Penguin Books Ltd.)
Penguin Group (Australia), 250 Camberwell Road, Camberwell, Victoria 3124,
Australia (a division of Pearson Australia Group Pty. Ltd.)
Penguin Books India Pvt. Ltd., 11 Community Centre, Panchsheel Park,
New Delhi - 110 017, India
Penguin Group (NZ), 67 Apollo Drive, Rosedale, North Shore 0632,
New Zealand (a division of Pearson New Zealand Ltd.)
Penguin Books (South Africa) (Pty.) Ltd., 24 Sturdee Avenue,
Rosebank, Johannesburg 2196, South Africa

Penguin Books Ltd., Registered Offices:
80 Strand, London WC2R 0RL, England

First published by Signet, an imprint of New American Library,
a division of Penguin Group (USA) Inc.

First Printing, February 2011
10 9 8 7 6 5 4 3 2 1

The first chapter of this book previously appeared in *Terror Town,* the three hundred
fifty-first volume in this series.

Copyright © Penguin Group (USA) Inc., 2011
All rights reserved

 REGISTERED TRADEMARK—MARCA REGISTRADA

Printed in the United States of America

The Trailsman

Beginnings . . . they bend the tree and they mark the man. Skye Fargo was born when he was eighteen. Terror was his midwife, vengeance his first cry. Killing spawned Skye Fargo, ruthless, cold-blooded murder. Out of the acrid smoke of gunpowder still hanging in the air, he rose, cried out a promise never forgotten.

The Trailsman they began to call him all across the West: searcher, scout, hunter, the man who could see where others only looked, his skills for hire but not his soul, the man who lived each day to the fullest, yet trailed each tomorrow. Skye Fargo, the Trailsman, the seeker who could take the wildness of a land and the wanting of a woman and make them his own.

The badlands of Texas, 1861—where death is always a heartbeat away.

1

There were so many buzzards that from far off they looked like a swarm of flies.

Skye Fargo was crossing the baked plains of central Texas when he spied the dark devourers of the dead in the pale blue sky. He could have ignored them and ridden on to Fort Lancaster. Instead, he reined the Ovaro toward them. He didn't know what he would find. It might be the remains of slaughtered buffalo. That many buzzards, there had to be a lot of dead.

Fargo was a tall man, broad of shoulder and narrow at the hip. He always wore buckskins, and was partial to a white hat and red bandanna. The buckskins were a clue to his stock-in-trade; he was a scout, and a good one. He knew the ways of the wild lands better than most any man alive, which was why he now put his hand on his Colt.

There had to be fifty of the big birds, their black wings outspread, their grotesque featherless heads as red as the blood of the kills they dined on.

Fargo climbed a low rise and drew rein. "Damn," he said to the empty air.

Five Conestogas were strung along the bank of a creek. They weren't moving. They couldn't; their teams had been taken. The canvas tops hung in strips. The belongings of those who owned the wagons were scattered all over, and scattered among the belongings were their bodies.

Fargo scanned the prairie. Other than the vultures, nothing moved. He gigged the Ovaro.

A particularly large buzzard was pecking at the eye socket of a dead woman. It plucked the eyeball out and gulped it with a flick of its long neck, then bent to the other eye.

Fargo shot it. At the blast, the buzzards feasting on other figures hissed and flapped to get airborne. One buzzard flew right at him and he raised the Colt but the bird banked and soared over his head.

Fargo came to a burly man in overalls whose throat had been ravaged by the beaks of the hungry birds. The man's eyes hadn't been touched. They were wide open and glazed and mirrored sheer horror.

Fargo climbed down. He held on to the reins as he went from body to body. Not that he had any doubts. A broken arrow told him who was to blame. They were thorough, the Comanches. He stepped over a grandfather clock, its mechanical innards strewn about. He moved amid pots and pans and clothes and tools. No weapons, though. The Comanches wouldn't leave those.

Fargo came to the body of a woman who had been cut from belly to neck. Her intestines had spilled out and one of her ears was missing.

A groan caused Fargo to stiffen. He went around a covered wagon. Near it lay a middle-aged man, twitching. The man had no clothes. Nor fingers or toes. His nose was missing. Incredibly, he was still alive. As Fargo came over, he blinked and licked his parched lips.

"Thank God."

Fargo squatted in a pool of dry blood. "I can get you to the fort if you want."

The man said something in a hoarse whisper.

"I didn't catch that," Fargo said, and bent his ear to the man's lips.

"Kill me."

Fargo straightened.

"Put me out of my misery. Please."

"There's a chance," Fargo said.

"No, there's not," the man replied. "I'm a goner and we both know it."

Fargo didn't say anything.

The man let out a sob. "They hit us out of nowhere just as it got dark. Twenty or more. We didn't even see them but we heard them whoop and holler. There wasn't time to circle the wagons."

"It wouldn't have helped," Fargo said. Not against that many.

"Half the men were down before the rest could lift a gun. I was in our wagon looking for the axle grease and my wife was driving or I'd have been killed outright too."

"The Comanches have been on a rampage lately," Fargo said. "No one knows why."

"Hell, mister. They don't need an excuse." The man coughed and blood trickled from a corner of his mouth.

"Would you like some water?"

"God, would I."

Fargo fetched his canteen. He opened it and carefully tilted it. The man gulped and sighed.

"I'm obliged."

"How many were in your party?" Fargo asked. He'd counted twelve bodies.

"Seventeen, counting me."

"Hell," Fargo said.

"They took four women. The youngest. Why them and not

anyone else I couldn't say. I heard them screaming as they were dragged off."

"Maybe the warriors took a shine to them." Fargo was being optimistic. A lot of tribes, the Apaches, for instance, thought white women were too puny to make good wives.

"You have to go after them. You have to save them."

"Twenty Comanches and one of me." Fargo didn't mind the high odds but twenty Comanches were twenty Comanches.

"Go to Fort Lancaster, then. Tell the colonel what happened. Tell him one of the women they took was his daughter, Miranda."

"Maybe you shouldn't talk. You might last longer."

"Who wants to last?" The man weakly grasped Fargo's sleeve. "I asked you before. I'm asking you again. Kill me."

Fargo had put horses out of their misery. And once a mule.

It was never a task he liked.

The man let out a ragged gasp. "Tell me you'll get word to the army."

"I'll get word."

The beating of heavy wings drew Fargo's gaze to the sky. More vultures were arriving. When he looked down, the man's eyes were empty of life. He felt for a pulse but there wasn't any.

Fargo checked the rest of the bodies. He noticed that every single one had been shot. Not one had been knifed or pierced by an arrow or transfixed by a lance. Yet there had been that broken arrow. When he was satisfied they were all dead he climbed on the Ovaro and roved in circles until he found where the attackers had gone off to the northwest.

He figured they had a good day and a half start on him, maybe more. As much as he wanted to help the women, he had to be realistic. Reluctantly, he reined around and tapped his spurs.

Behind him, the dark legion descended.

2

Fort Lancaster was situated on Live Oak Creek not far from where the creek flowed into the Pecos River. As forts went, it was impressive. Two dozen buildings were arranged around a spacious parade ground. Among them were a sutler's and a bakery, a blacksmith shop and a hospital.

Fargo rode up to the headquarters. He dismounted and tied the Ovaro to the hitch rail. Brushing dust from his buckskins he climbed the steps.

A young orderly sat at a desk, scribbling. His uniform was clean and pressed. "Yes, sir?"

"I'd like to see the colonel."

Before the orderly could respond, an officer came out of a side office. He was tall and thin-boned and had a stiff bearing. "I'm Major Hargrove. Who are you and what do you want to see Colonel Crowley about?"

Fargo didn't like the man's tone. "It's for his ears, not yours."

"We expect him back tomorrow. You can leave word with the orderly if you refuse to tell me." Major Hargrove sounded offended.

"Does he have a daughter named Miranda?"

"That he does," the major confirmed. "A fine girl. She was the darling of the detachment but she went and married a farmer." The way he said "farmer" was the way some people would say "cur." "What about her?"

6

Fargo decided he might as well. He told him about the wagons and the bodies.

Hargrove grew red in the face as he listened. "Those stinking, filthy savages," he rasped when Fargo finished. "The colonel will be heartbroken."

"I'll come see him tomorrow."

"Hold on there," Major Hargrove said, and grabbed Fargo's arm. "Where do you think you're going?"

"To get a bite to eat and have a few drinks and sleep for ten hours."

"I'm calling out the men and you'll lead us to where you found the wagons."

"No." Fargo shrugged loose of his grip.

"What the hell do you mean, no?"

"Major, I rode two days and two nights to get here. I'm worn-out and so is my horse. We need rest."

"But those women—"

"They were taken four days ago. Another night won't make a difference."

Hargrove gave it some thought. "No, I suppose you're right. It wouldn't do to go charging off. By now they are deep in Comanche country." He smacked his right fist against his left palm. "But damn, I hate to think of that sweet girl in the hands of those filthy redskins."

"What time do you expect the colonel?"

"He should be here by noon at the latest."

Fargo nodded and opened the door.

"Wait. I didn't catch your name."

Fargo told him and went out. Troopers on horseback were on the parade ground drilling and dust hung heavy over them and their mounts.

A quarter of a mile off stood a cluster of buildings. There were saloons and a feed and grain and not much else.

7

Fargo stopped at the first watering hole. The Tumbleweed smelled of liquor and tobacco and was practically empty. He took a corner table and sat with his back to the wall.

A shapely dove in a blue dress sashayed over. She had big eyes almost as blue as his and a saucy quirk to her red lips. "What's your poison, you handsome devil?"

"That sign says you serve food," Fargo said, with a bob of his head. "Any chance of a steak and potatoes?"

"We're short on beef so the steak will be venison. We always have potatoes." She leaned on the table and smiled. "Anything else you need, you just ask. They call me Bunny, by the way."

"Because you have big ears or a cute tail?"

Bunny laughed. "Because when I was little I hopped around all over the place." She stood back. "The food will take about fifteen minutes. What would you like in the meantime?"

"The best whiskey you have." Fargo figured he should treat himself after more than a week without.

"Are you with the army? You look to me like you might be a scout."

"I'm between jobs," Fargo said. As she turned, he gave her a light swat. "Look me up later. I could use some company."

"Oh, could you?" Bunny said, and grinned. "Maybe I will and maybe I won't." Her bottom jiggled as she walked away.

Fargo leaned back. A night of fun and frolic was just what he needed to help him forget the wagon train. He took out his poke. He had seventeen dollars to his name, enough for the meal and the bottle and to sit in on a few hands of poker.

Bunny brought the whiskey and a glass. She contrived to stand close so when she put them down her hip rubbed his arm.

"The more I look at you, the more I like what I see."

8

"Does that mean we're on for tonight?"

"I'll let you know when I've made up my mind." Bunny touched a finger to his beard. "I doubt many girls tell you no." She playfully pinched his cheek and went to wait on another customer.

When his food came, Fargo dug in. The venison was thick and juicy; the potatoes were smeared in butter. There were also string beans. He washed everything down with whiskey and by the time he pushed his plate back, he felt full and fine.

Outside, night was on the cusp of descending. The saloon had filled. The noise level rose: the hubbub of voices, the clink of glasses and chips.

Fargo was debating which poker table to join when trouble started.

Usually saloon fights were over an insult or because someone cheated at cards or someone *thought* someone cheated at cards. This one started when someone bumped Bunny and the tray she was carrying slipped. A glass of beer tipped and splashed onto a big trooper's neck and shoulders. Bellowing like a mad bull, the trooper heaved out of his chair and shoved Bunny so hard she pitched against a chair.

"What in hell do you think you're doing, you stupid cow?"

Fargo's legs seemed to have a mind of their own. He was at Bunny's side helping her stand while everyone else stood rooted in surprise. "Are you all right?"

"Yes, thank you," Bunny said. The beer had spilled on her, too, and the front of her dress was wet.

A heavy hand fell on Fargo's shoulder and he was spun around.

"You a friend of this cow's?" the big trooper growled.

"I wish you wouldn't call me that," Bunny said.

"I'll call you any damn thing I please."

"It was an accident," Bunny explained. "Someone bumped me."

"I should slap you silly. Look at me. I smell like a brewery."

"You have another problem besides how you smell," Fargo said.

"What might that be?"

"Me," Fargo said, and hit him.

3

Fargo smashed the trooper flush on the chin and rocked him onto his heels. For a moment Fargo thought the man would go down but the trooper recovered, rubbed his chin, and did the last thing Fargo expected—the trooper grinned.

"Not bad."

"Hell," Fargo said.

Gamblers and drinkers were scrambling to get elsewhere. In a twinkling the nearest chairs were empty and a ring of excited onlookers had formed.

"Pound him, Corporal Brunk!"

The trooper balled his fists. "This is going to be fun. I haven't got to pound on anyone in a while."

Fargo set himself and raised his fists. "You're welcome to try."

Corporal Brunk shoved his chair out of the way and pushed the table to one side. "I've beaten more men than you have fingers and toes."

"You can count that high?"

Brunk came in swinging. He was big and heavy and ponderous. Fargo easily blocked and dodged several looping swings but he didn't see the boot that caught him on the hip. The blow knocked him against a table and chips clattered. As he recovered his balance Brunk was on him. He slipped a cross and landed a powerful right to the cheek. Brunk grunted and came in again. Slowly giving way, Fargo let the trooper tire himself with swing after swing.

Brunk was strong but he lacked stamina. He commenced to breathe heavily and to grunt with each swing.

Fargo was tired. He'd had a long day. He hoped to end the fight quickly by unleashing a straight-arm with all his weight and power behind it. He twisted at the hips for extra force. His knuckles exploded against Brunk's jaw and the trooper swayed. Fargo cocked his arm to finish it when suddenly someone in uniform was between them, a hand against his chest.

It was Major Hargrove. "That will be quite enough, the both of you."

Brunk glowered over the officer's shoulder at Fargo. "I didn't start it, Major. This peckerwood did."

"That's right!" someone hollered.

"Like hell!" another declared. "Brunk started it when he pushed poor Bunny."

"All I did was spill some beer," Bunny said.

Major Hargrove motioned for quiet. "No one ever agrees on how these brawls start. Frankly, I don't care. Corporal Brunk, you will consider yourself on report. You are to return to the post immediately."

"Ah, hell," Brunk said.

"You're aware of the regulations," Major Hargrove said. "This isn't the first time your temper has gotten you into trouble."

"It's not fair."

"Tell it to the colonel tomorrow."

Grumbling, Corporal Brunk wheeled and barreled through the onlookers like an ox through reeds. Those who didn't get out of his way quickly enough were shoved aside.

"Friendly bastard," Fargo said.

Major Hargrove shrugged. "Say what you will, he's a good soldier when he hasn't been drinking. There's none braver in this man's army."

"He shouldn't have shoved me," Bunny said. "It was an accident, me spilling that beer on him."

"Be that as it may," Hargrove said coldly, "you're hardly fit to cast stones, given what you do for a living."

"I serve drinks."

"If that were all you served I wouldn't object to your existence." The major wheeled and strode ramrod-straight out the batwings.

"Object to my existence?" Bunny said. "Who talks like that? Was he saying I'm better off dead?" She didn't wait for Fargo to answer. "He's a strange one, that major. He comes in for a drink now and then but he never shows any interest in the ladies."

"Never trust a man who isn't fond of petticoats," Fargo said.

Bunny laughed. "Speaking of which, for your gallantry you can escort me home. We close at midnight."

"That early?" Fargo had looked forward to playing cards until the wee hours.

"Blame the army, not us. All the soldiers have to be back at the fort by midnight and without them the saloons don't make much money."

"Midnight it is."

Tables and chairs were being replaced and card games were being resumed. Fargo chose an empty chair and got out his poke. He lost the first few hands and then his luck changed. He didn't win much but he stayed ahead and that was the important thing. Now and again Bunny strolled by and put a hand on his shoulder or rubbed his ear or his neck.

The bartender bellowed that it was last call.

Fargo looked around. Most of the soldiers were filing out, and they didn't look happy about it. He was dealt his last hand. Two queens, two tens and a two. He asked for a card and it was another queen. His face carved in stone, he called and then raised and then raised again and raked in his biggest pot. He was jingling the coins in his poke when a warm hand caressed his cheek.

"Did good, did you?" Bunny said.

"No complaints." Fargo pushed his chair back and she pressed against him.

"You still want to escort me home?"

"Depends."

"On what?"

"When we get there, do I have to peel your clothes off by myself or will you help?"

Tittering, Bunny said, "It seems to be your night for playing your cards right. I reckon I can help."

Fargo cupped her bottom.

"Not here," Bunny squealed. She pulled him to the batwings and out into the cool of the night. They'd taken only a couple of steps when a dark shape blocked their path.

"I've been waiting for you," Corporal Brunk said.

4

Bunny had spunk. She poked the corporal in the chest and said, "The major told you to go to the fort."

"I did. And snuck back."

"You leave us be, you hear?"

"I'm not here for you," Brunk said, and shoved her. "I'm here for him."

A fist arced at Fargo. He barely avoided it. Pivoting, he drove knuckles into Brunk's gut and Brunk took a step back.

Quickly, Fargo unleashed a flurry to the stomach and the chin. Brunk was tough; he absorbed the blows and rammed two overhands. Fargo ducked the first but the second clipped him on the shoulder. Pain shot clear down his arm. He avoided a looping right, scored with two quick jabs, and lost his hat to a swing that would have taken his head off. Bunny was yelling for Brunk to stop. Rumbling deep in his chest, the corporal closed and flung fist after fist. Brunk relied on his size and brute strength. Most of the time that was probably enough but Fargo was as strong if not as big, and Fargo was considerably quicker. For every blow Brunk landed, Fargo landed three or four. They slugged and countered and slipped and just when it seemed the fight would go on half the night, Brunk missed and overextended, putting his jaw practically in front of Fargo's face, and Fargo brought his right fist up from down around his knees. The crack of his knuckles on

Brunk's jaw was like the crack of a hammer on a walnut shell. Brunk tilted onto his toes, teetered, and keeled back with his arms out. He hit the street with a thud, raising puffs of dust, and was still.

"I'll be damned," someone said.

"Knocked him plumb out," marveled another.

"Never thought I'd see the day anyone could do that to Orville Brunk," a third man remarked.

Fargo was sore and bruised and his shoulder hurt like hell. He was tempted to stave in a few of the corporal's ribs with a few well-placed kicks but he refrained and picked up his hat.

Bunny's warm hand slipped into his. "You were wonderful."

"He was tough," Fargo said.

"None tougher, or so they say," Bunny replied. She looked down at the sprawled form. "Didn't do him much good against you though."

"Folks say I'm tough too."

"You sure are." Bunny brightened and pulled on his arm. "Let's go. We can't let that lunkhead spoil our mood." She led him down the street. Frame houses lined both sides. Most were small and without the frills of a fence or a flower bed. A path brought them to a porch. She produced a key, put a finger to her lips to enjoin quiet, and opened the door. As she closed it she whispered, "I'm not the only boarder. We can't make a whole lot of noise."

The stairs creaked under their weight. She produced another key and ushered him into her room. It was like the house, small and quaint. There was a bed and a table and chair and a washstand and a chest of drawers. It left little space to move around.

Bunny closed the door and put her back to it and grinned.

"Now then," she teased. "What did you have in mind?"

"This." Fargo molded his body to hers and felt the soft twin cushions of her breasts press his chest. Her fingers found the back of his neck as his mouth found her lips. Her tongue was velvet sugar. She was a good kisser. Her breath and her body warmed. He cupped a breast and then the other. She ground herself into his groin and softly moaned. To his delight, her fingers enfolded his pole.

"Goodness, you're fine," she breathed in his ear.

"You're not a talker, are you?" One of Fargo's peeves was women who gabbed while they made love. Hen chatter was for sewing circles and church socials, not the bed.

"Not me," Bunny whispered, and proved it by sucking on his lip.

Fargo guided her around the table and past the chair to the bed. It was small like everything else and when he stretched out his boots were over the end.

"Be careful of those spurs," Bunny cautioned.

Fargo sat up and shed his boots and gun belt. He gave himself over to the pleasure of her body. Her dress had only a few buttons and would have been easy to shed except that it fit so tight he almost had to rip it off. When he had her naked he took a few moments to lean on his elbow and admire the cream of her skin and run his hand from her shoulder to her thigh.

"Like what you see?"

"A lot."

"Less eyeballing and more groping, if you please," Bunny requested, and giggled.

"You're a playful minx," Fargo complimented her.

"I am a girl who likes her fun."

"Works out real well," Fargo said. "I am a guy who likes girls."

"Now who is gabbing?" Bunny said.

That was the last of the talk for a while. Fargo kneaded and caressed and tweaked while she cooed and rubbed and dug her fingernails into his shoulders. At length he slid a hand between her silken thighs and rubbed her wet furnace. She shivered and bit him. He inserted a finger to the knuckle. Her inner walls rippled and she humped his hand. He kept at the foreplay until she was panting. He shed his pants. Parting her legs, he slid into position. He brushed her slit with his redwood.

"God, yes," Bunny whispered. "Do me. Do me hard."

Fargo was happy to oblige. She was wild and wanton but quiet at it. The bed slapped the floor and he wondered how the other boarders couldn't help but hear, and then he was at the crest and didn't give a good damn. Their explosion was mutual. They coasted to a sweat-caked stop and he eased off her heaving chest and lay at her side.

"I love it," Bunny said dreamily. "I could do this every night of my life."

"You and me both," Fargo said.

5

Fargo no sooner reined to a stop at the hitch rail in front of the headquarters the next day when the door flew open and out strode an angry Major Hargrove.

"Where the hell have you been? It's almost noon."

Unflustered, Fargo dismounted and looped the reins. "You told me he wouldn't be here until then."

"He arrived earlier than we expected." The major impatiently motioned. "He's anxious to talk to you."

"I'll bet."

The orderly and a captain stopped talking when Fargo entered. Hargrove held the door to the colonel's office. Spartan, clean and polished, it was the kind of office most people would imagine a fort commander to have. The commander was another story.

Colonel Crowley was a plump pumpkin with a ruddy complexion and no chin to speak of. His eyes were pools of worry and he was gnawing on his lower lip. Rising, he offered his hand. "Fargo, is it? I've heard of you. General McAllister says you are one of the finest scouts alive."

Fargo shook. It was like shaking a limp cloth. "I've worked with him a few times."

Crowley gestured at a chair. "Have a seat, if you don't mind. Can I have the orderly bring you anything? Coffee? Tea, perhaps?"

"Have any whiskey?"

"I'm afraid not. This is a military installation, after all."

"Colonel," Major Hargove said.

Crowley glanced at him. "Yes. Of course." He sank into his chair with his fingers in a tepee on the desk. "I've been informed that you think my daughter was abducted."

"There's no 'think' about it," Fargo said. "She was taken along with three other women."

"And you didn't go after them?"

"They had too much of a start, and I figured I should report it."

"From what I understand you spent all night— How shall I put this? Carousing?"

"Put it any way you want."

Colonel Crowley sat back and made another tepee on his round chest. "I must say, your cavalier attitude upsets me. Instead of being here waiting for me, you were off in bed with a strumpet."

"A nice strumpet," Fargo said.

"Please. Your dalliances are your affair. My concern is my daughter. A concern you evidently don't share."

"I came to let you know, didn't I?"

"Yes. Yes, you did. Very well. We'll drop that for the time being. Of paramount importance now is to find her abductors."

"Don't you mean find *her*?" Fargo said.

"Naturally." Crowley returned the tepee to his desk. "Be ready to leave in fifteen minutes. Major Hargrove and forty troopers should be enough to deal with the war party."

"You're not coming?"

"I'm in charge of Fort Lancaster. I can hardly go riding off and desert my duties."

Fargo wasn't shocked often but this did. "She's your daughter."

"I appreciate that," Colonel Crowley said. "As you must appreciate my position."

Major Hargrove came around the desk and stood at the colonel's elbow. "The scout has a point, sir."

"Eh? He does?"

"It wouldn't look good for you to sit here and leave it all to us."

"It wouldn't?"

"No, sir. As the scout pointed out, she's your flesh and blood. Washington would think it curious."

"They're not the only ones," Fargo said to Crowley. "What the hell is wrong with you?"

"I beg your pardon?"

Major Hargrove frowned. "I'll thank you not to address the colonel in that tone. There are issues here you can't possibly understand."

"Try me," Fargo said.

"I will not," Colonel Crowley said. "You are dismissed. Get whatever supplies you need."

"You're forgetting something," Fargo said. "I'm not signed on with the army at the moment. I'm a civilian. I can do as I damn well please."

"But you said you would guide the patrol to the wagons."

"And I will." Fargo stood. "But if you want something, ask. Don't boss me around like you have the right."

The captain was still by the orderly's desk and when Fargo went past, trailed out after him. "I'd like a word with you, Mr. Fargo, if you don't mind."

Fargo was about to cross to the sutler's. "Have it while we walk."

"I'm your new best friend," the captain said.

Stopping so abruptly the officer nearly collided with him, Fargo said, "Say that so it makes sense."

The captain had curly blond hair and a short trimmed mustache and an angular face bronzed by the sun. His uniform was speckled with dust and his boots were scuffed. "Major Hargrove ordered me to glue myself to you. His very words."

"I have enough friends," Fargo said, and walked on.

The captain quickly caught up. "Don't take it personal. I'm only following orders." He smiled and thrust out a hand. "James Baker, from Toledo, Ohio."

Despite himself, Fargo took a liking to the man. "What if I tell you to get lost?"

"I follow you around like a long-lost puppy until you get mad and break my jaw. Then I get relieved from duty for a month and treat myself to cards and liquor every night."

"A man after my own heart," Fargo said. "What makes you think I'd break your jaw?"

"You're twice as big as me, and from what I've heard, not a gent to be trifled with."

Fargo liked him even more. "You can be my pup on one condition."

"I don't own a leash," Captain Baker said.

Fargo chuckled. "Explain your colonel to me. His daughter is taken and he wants to sit on his fat ass behind his desk and let others go find her?"

Baker coughed and gazed at the headquarters and looked down at his scuffed boots. "Off the record?"

"I don't have a pencil and paper."

Now it was the captain who chuckled. "Our esteemed commanding officer isn't the army's ideal of a true soldier."

"No fooling."

"He's"—Captain Baker paused as if searching for the right word—"timid."

"Hell," Fargo said.

"He wasn't always," Captain Baker said. "They say he lost

his nerve in a fight with the Apaches. Saw his best friend gutted before his eyes."

Fargo tried to imagine the bowl of mush behind the desk battling the most fierce warriors anywhere.

"The colonel hasn't been the same since. Major Hargrove does most of the day-to-day commanding, if you will."

"Hargrove is his backbone," Fargo said.

"You don't mince words." Captain Baker nodded. "But more or less, yes." He motioned at the sprawl of buildings. "Appearances to the contrary, Fort Lancaster isn't considered a prime post. Truth is, there's talk it will be shut down in a year or so."

"So the army tucked Crowley away here, where he can't do much harm," Fargo guessed.

"They tucked Major Hargrove, too," Captain Baker said.

"He's got a backbone."

"But not a lot of discretion." Captain Baker hesitated again. "The major has been reprimanded twice for needlessly exposing those under him to danger. Unduly reckless is how it's described in the official report. He also hates Indians with every particle of his being." Captain Baker grinned. "So you have a coward and a bigot about to lead us off against the Comanches."

"Son of a bitch," Fargo said.

6

The column raised a lot of dust. It couldn't be helped. The forty troopers rode four abreast. The creak of leather and the clank of accoutrements was near continuous. Watching them, it made Fargo think of a giant centipede scuttling across the prairie.

At his side rode Captain Baker. A good rider, the young officer had an air of competence about him.

The same couldn't be said of Colonel Crowley. Fargo nearly laughed every time he glanced over his shoulder. Crowley flopped and flapped and tilted to one side of the saddle or the other in the most god-awful display of horsemanship he'd ever seen.

"They shouldn't let him out from behind a desk," Fargo said at one point.

Baker didn't bother to look back. "Another reason the colonel didn't want to come. His daughter or not, he can't stand to embarrass himself."

"Then he should stay away from horses."

"Hard to do when you're in the cavalry."

Fort Lancaster was two days behind them. It was the middle of the morning and the temperature was already pushing one hundred. Fargo was used to the heat but a lot of the troopers—most of them boys who had yet to see their twentieth birthday—were grimly holding up the best they could.

"How much farther?" Captain Baker asked.

Fargo pointed at black specks high in the sky in the distance.

"They're still feeding after all this time?" Captain Baker said.

"They had a lot to feed on."

Baker puckered his mouth. "Tell me true. What do you think our chances are?"

"Depends on what they do with the women," Fargo said.

"Comanches mostly use them and kill them, don't they? Or maybe take them for a wife."

"If," Fargo said.

"If what?"

"I'll tell you when we get there."

Not much had changed. The wagons stood stark and abandoned on the slow decay to ruin. The pools of blood, once vivid scarlet, were now black. As for the bodies, the buzzards had gorged on the feast of rotting flesh and most were gleaming bones. The stench was abominable.

Fargo pulled his bandanna up over his mouth and nose.

The skull of the farmer who had told him about the women grinned up at him as if dying were a great joke.

Captain Baker had a hand over the lower half of his face. "God Almighty," he said through his fingers.

Colonel Crowley and Major Hargrove drew rein. The colonel was fit to gag and kept taking deep breaths and holding them. The major hardly seemed to notice the reek.

"Stinking savages. All these poor people dead, on account of a bunch of red animals."

"You would think that," Fargo said.

"Don't tell me you're an Indian lover," Major Hargrove said.

"I've lived with a couple of tribes," Fargo said. It was

25

more than a couple but he wasn't in the habit of sharing his personal life. "They're people just like us."

"The hell they are." Major Hargrove spat. "Look around you. Would whites do something like this? An atrocity so vile?"

"They did," Fargo said.

The major and the colonel looked at one another and the colonel said, "I beg your pardon?"

"All of them were shot," Fargo said.

Hargrove leaned on his saddle horn. "So?"

"So Comanches have guns but not that many. They use bows and arrows. They use lances and knives." Fargo nodded at the black lake of skeletons. "Not one I saw was cut. Not one was stabbed. Not one body had an arrow sticking in it or a hole where an arrow had been pulled out."

Colonel Crowley gulped more foul air. "Are you suggesting that white men were to blame?"

"I'm not suggesting," Fargo said. "I'm saying."

"Bullshit," Major Hargrove said. "You told us that the farmer told you they were Comanches. Now we're to believe you over him?"

"Believe whatever you want," Fargo said. "I've got a hundred dollars in my poke that says their skin was as white as yours."

"I'm on duty," Hargrove said. "I can't gamble even if I had the habit, which I don't."

"Hold on a minute," Colonel Crowley said. "Let me see if I follow this. You're saying that white men dressed as Indians wiped out the wagon train and took four women and only four women, among them my daughter."

"They took the youngest."

"Is that significant?"

"Has to be or they'd have taken others." Fargo realized he

must make each particular perfectly clear. "They dressed as Indians to shift the blame and throw whoever came after them off the scent."

"Bullshit," Major Hargrove said again. "You said it yourself: The Comanches have rifles."

"In a war party of twenty there might be four or five rifles," Fargo said. "The rest would use bows and lances."

"I don't know," Colonel Crowley said, gazing perplexedly about.

"There's one way to find out," Fargo said. "We catch the sons of bitches."

"After all this time?" Colonel Crowley said.

"If they were Comanches, no," Fargo said. "Whites, we have a chance."

"Listen to you," Major Hargrove scoffed. "As if the redskins are so much better than us."

"Comanches are taught to ride as soon as they can walk. Most of your command are boys fresh off the farm or city born."

"They can fight as good as any damn Comanches," Major Hargrove said.

Fargo let that pass. To the colonel he said, "A week at the most and we'll overtake them." Provided it didn't rain, he reflected.

"A week in the saddle?" Crowley said bleakly.

"It's your daughter they took," Fargo reminded him.

"Yes, it is, isn't it?" Colonel Crowley bobbed his chinless head. "We push on, then, as fast as we must." He raised his fist in what he thought must be a fierce gesture. "And the devil take the hindmost."

"God help us," Fargo said.

7

The flatland brought them to rolling hills. At twilight they pitched camp. Everything ran with the usual military efficiency. The horses were picketed and fires were kindled and sentries posted and the troopers were allowed to relax.

Fargo was seated cross-legged across a fire from Captain Baker, sipping coffee, when someone came up.

"Remember me?" Corporal Brunk said.

"Hard to forget a slab of muscle as big as you," Fargo said.

Brunk grinned. "Didn't know if you'd spotted me."

"I did," Fargo said.

"You scouts don't miss much, do you?"

"It'd be like missing a redwood," Fargo said.

"Those big trees? Where is it they grow? California? Have you been out there?"

"I've been everywhere."

"Must be nice. I wanted to see more of the world. It's why I joined the army." Brunk gazed about the encampment. "Mostly all I see are uniforms and the hind ends of horses."

"You making small talk or what?"

"Just wanted to give my regards." Brunk turned to go. "I admire a man who can whup me."

Captain Baker had been listening. "The two of you fought, Corporal?" he asked in mild astonishment.

Brunk nodded. "First time I've ever been knocked out. This son of a bitch is all they say he is." He nodded at Fargo and walked off.

"Peculiar man," Captain Baker said. He studied Fargo. "Iron hard, too. He has never, to my knowledge, come close to being beaten."

Fargo shrugged.

"When he's sober he's about the best soldier in our command," Captain Baker said. "When he's drunk—" Now it was Baker who shrugged.

"His respect was genuine?"

"I'd say so, yes. Brunk lives by his own code. The tougher someone is, the more highly he thinks of them."

"He must respect the hell out of Colonel Crowley."

Baker started to laugh and caught himself.

"Did I hear my name mentioned?" the commanding officer asked as he eased down with all the grace of a dumpling.

With him was Major Hargrove. Hargrove stood with his hands clasped behind his back in a parade-rest posture. "Was Corporal Brunk giving you trouble?"

"We were passing the time of day," Fargo said.

"If he does you let me know. I'll deal with him."

"I stomp my own snakes," Fargo said.

Colonel Crowley rested his elbows on his legs and his chinless head in his hands. "It's been a long day, gentlemen. I am so sore I can hardly sit. Why do saddles have to be so uncomfortable?"

"Depends on how you sit them," Fargo said.

"I have never been able to ride all that well," Colonel Crowley said. "Perhaps you noticed."

"You're the worst rider I've ever seen," Fargo bluntly responded.

"Here now," Major Hargrove said.

"No, it's all right," Colonel Crowley said. "I appreciate his honesty. I've never denied I'm terrible at it. I've tried and tried but I can't do it well at all."

"You sit too far front," Fargo told him. "Your weight should be on your ass and your back, not your belly."

"I do tend to lean a little forward." Crowley smiled. "Thank you for the advice." He pushed his hat back. "But on to more serious matters. Do you still insist we are after white men?"

"I do."

"They must be outlaws. Texas is infested with their violent breed. I daresay that west Texas has become a virtual haven for their kind. There is little law and the army's presence is minimal."

"I still say it could be Comanches," Major Hargrove interjected.

"We'll find out soon enough," Colonel Crowley said. "I'm not resting until my sweet Miranda is safely back at the post."

Fargo didn't mention that his sweet Miranda might in fact be dead.

Colonel Crowley gazed at the stars. "I've never been all that fond of the outdoors but moments like this, I almost like it."

"You don't like the outdoors and you enlisted in the army?" Fargo said.

"Most of what I do, I do from behind a desk. To be frank, I like it that way. I like my comforts."

"And your food."

Crowley laughed. "Eating is the one thing I do extremely well." He patted his bulging gut. "My superiors are not all that pleased with me, but a pie is a pie." He cocked his head. "Is there nothing in this world you can't do without, Mr. Fargo?"

"Women. Whiskey. My horse," Fargo answered.

"With me it has always been food. A terrible thing to admit but there you have it."

Fargo was almost beginning to like him. "At least you're honest about it."

"I may be the world's worst rider and awfully out of shape but yes, I am honest with myself, if nothing else."

Major Hargrove coughed. "You don't have to tell him all this, sir. It's none of his damn business."

"To the contrary," Colonel Crowley said. "He's our tracker. My daughter's life is in his hands. I see no reason not to be friendly."

Hargrove's expression reminded Fargo of a man he once saw eating a lemon.

Over at another fire a sergeant called out that the stew was ready.

Colonel Crowley brightened and quickly rose. "At last. I suppose I'll have to limit myself to two bowls. That's the worst part of being out in the field. The fare is abominable."

He departed with his sinister shadow.

"The fare," Fargo said.

"He tries," Captain Baker said, and chuckled. "You have to admit we're a colorful outfit."

"Mostly green boys and a commanding officer who should have been a cook."

"What are you saying?"

"We're heading into the badlands where it's kill or be killed."

"If you were in my boots, would you be worried for our men?"

"Were I in your boots," Fargo said, "I'd be worried as hell."

8

They struck the cross trail the next afternoon. Fargo drew rein and dismounted. He was on a knee, the reins in his hand, when the rest of the column clattered to a stop.

"What have you found, scout?" Colonel Crowley asked.

Fargo nodded at the tracks. "Five unshod horses."

"More whites pretending to be savages?" Major Hargrove said sarcastically.

"These are the real article," Fargo said. "Comanches, a hunting party, maybe. They came from the west, saw the tracks we've been following, and went off to the east in a hurry."

"Why in a hurry?" Colonel Crowley said.

Fargo straightened. "I think they have the same idea we do. They're going to get more warriors and go after the bunch we're after."

"Or it could be," Major Hargrove sneered, "that the ones we're after are in fact Comanches and the ones who came on their trail are from another tribe and got the hell out of here."

"That's reasonable, isn't it?" Colonel Crowley said.

"But unlikely," Fargo said. "Most tribes fight shy of Comanche territory."

"Be that as it may, I deem it worth investigating." Crowley turned to Hargrove. "Major, take ten men and go after the five Indians." He glanced at Fargo. "How long ago would you say they went by?"

"Not more than a couple of hours."

"Excellent. Then the major won't have any trouble catching up to them."

Captain Baker cleared his throat. "And what is the major to do when he does, sir?"

"I'll leave that up to the major," Colonel Crowley said. "If they're hostiles, he is to deal with them accordingly. If they are from a friendly tribe, he will let them be."

"You're making a mistake," Fargo said.

"Why don't you go with them?" Colonel Crowley suggested. "You know Indians better than any of us."

Major Hargrove didn't like that. "I'd rather he didn't, sir. I don't need a tracker to follow a trail this fresh."

"I insist," the colonel said.

Hargrove chose Corporal Brunk and nine troopers. They peeled from the column and prepared to ride off.

"Well?" Colonel Crowley said to Fargo. "Will you or won't you?"

Fargo stared at the nine boys in their ill-fitting uniforms, each sitting tall and proud in the saddle. "Hell." He climbed on the Ovaro.

"We'll find a suitable spot to camp and wait for you," Colonel Crowley said. "You shouldn't have any trouble finding us."

"Keep your eyes skinned," Fargo said. He gigged the Ovaro and acquired a shadow. "You too?"

"My orders are where you go, I go," Captain Baker said. "Besides, I wouldn't miss this for the world."

Fargo alternated between a trot and a walk so as not to tire their animals more than was necessary. He secretly hoped dark would fall before they caught up and that those they were after would spot their campfire and escape into the night.

But an hour before sunset a pinpoint of orange light in a

stretch of open country brought his hope crashing down. The Indians had stopped early.

"We're in luck," Major Hargrove said when the soldiers drew rein. "We'll wait for the sun to set and sneak up on them and surround their camp."

"You're going to sneak up on Comanches?" Fargo said.

"Don't come if you don't want to." Hargrove twisted in the saddle. "Corporal, see to it that each man's carbine is loaded and that canteens and anything else that might make noise and give us away are left behind."

"Yes, sir," Brunk said.

Time crawled. Fargo squatted apart from the others. He was in no mood for talk but Captain Baker wouldn't let it drop.

"Why are you so mad? We're fairly good at what we do."

"Comanches are more than fair."

"There are thirteen of us and five of them. We make up in numbers what we lack in skill."

"Keep thinking that."

"Maybe they'll hear us and run."

"Maybe they'll hear you and fight."

The gray of twilight darkened. Stars sparkled and a crescent of moon appeared. A coyote yipped and was answered by another.

Major Hargrove had been excitedly pacing but now he stopped and faced his men. "Pay attention. I don't want any mistakes. Be as quiet as you can. We'll advance by twos until I give the order to spread out in a skirmish line. We will surround them and close in. No one is to talk above a whisper." He paused. "Anyone have a question?"

"Why not let me go talk to them alone?" Fargo proposed.

"Do you speak Comanche?"

"Some."

"Isn't that interesting. What good would it do, though, you talking to them?"

"It could avoid bloodshed."

"That will be up to the savages. And since, as you've pointed out, you're a civilian, I prefer that you stay with the horses."

"No," Fargo said.

Hargrove hissed through his teeth. "Very well. But the same applies to you. Not a sound. And you will stay behind us so that you're not caught in any cross fire. The colonel wouldn't like that."

Fargo didn't like it, either, but he held his tongue.

When the soldiers moved out he came after them, Captain Baker at his side.

"For what it's worth," Baker whispered, "I'd have let you go talk."

Half a mile was a lot of ground to cover. The troopers went slowly and carefully but they rustled the grass and brushed against the brush and a few times someone stumbled or tripped.

Major Hargrove brought them to a halt a hundred yards from the fire. Five figures were huddled around it, eating and talking.

Fargo moved up to Hargrove. "I told you they were Comanches. Let me go speak to them."

"How can you tell which tribe from here?" Hargrove said. "And no, I won't. This is a military operation and you will stop interfering." He gave the command and his men quietly fanned out, their faces pale, their bodies rigid with dread.

Fargo had done all he could. He stayed where he was. Baker stayed with him.

The troopers moved as stealthily as they could, but they were forty yards out when a warrior at the fire stood and peered into the night.

"Uh-oh," Captain Baker said.

The Comanche who had stood said something and the others leaped up. In the bat of an eye they were out of the firelight and in the dark. A horse whinnied.

"After them, men!" Major Hargrove bellowed. "Don't let them get away!"

The troopers became rabbits, hopping and running. Carbines blasted. War whoops pierced the air. A trooper screamed and clutched a feathered shaft that jutted from his chest and collapsed. More guns boomed. Another man shrieked, his leg pierced. A third fell near the fire, a lance through his torso, convulsing violently. Then hooves drummed, rapidly fading. A few final whoops were raised in mockery. After that there was silence save for the cries of the dying and the wounded.

"Well, that went well," Captain Baker said.

Disgust filled Fargo. "Stupid is as stupid does." He began to back away unnoticed and when he had gone a dozen steps he turned and jogged. Behind him the captain shouted.

"Hey! Wait for me."

Fargo needed to reach the horses and slip away before Hargrove could try to stop him. He ran faster.

9

The Comanches didn't go far. When they were sure the soldiers hadn't given chase they circled to the south and approached to within an arrow's flight of Major Hargrove and his men. Two of the troopers had died and a third was being bandaged. The man wouldn't stop blubbering.

"My leg! God in heaven, look at the hole in my leg. Why won't it stop bleeding?"

"Hush, Private Newsome," the major commanded. "Comport yourself as a man."

"But it hurts!" the young private wailed.

The Comanches sat and watched. They made no move to use their weapons. They might have been statues, the warriors and their mounts.

A crude bandage staunched the bleeding of the trooper with the hurt leg. He was placed on his horse, and at a command from Major Hargrove, the troopers started back. They had no idea the Comanches were so close.

Fargo did. The drum of hooves smothered the sounds the Ovaro made as he brought the stallion to within ten yards of the Comanches. So intent were they on their enemies that their sharp senses failed them.

The five warriors didn't move until quiet reclaimed the night. At a word from the oldest, they rode to their campfire and climbed down. One of them touched a finger to a puddle of blood and said something that made the others laugh. Hunkering around the fire, they talked about how they had outwitted the bluecoats.

Fargo slid down. The reins in his left hand, his right palm out inches from his Colt, he stepped into the firelight.

It was rare for Comanches to be startled. Jumping up, they brandished their weapons.

"I am not your enemy," Fargo said.

A young warrior raised a bow and sighted down a shaft but lowered it when the oldest of them said, "No, Sparrow Hawk. He could have killed some of us but he did not. We will hear what he has to say."

"Thank you," Fargo said.

"I am Bull Running," the oldest warrior said. "How are you known?"

"The Minneconjou call me He Who Follows Many Trails."

"You are with the bluecoats?"

"I did not attack you," Fargo said. "I told them it was wrong but they would not listen."

One of the young warriors spoke quietly to Bull Running, who grunted. "Why should we believe you?"

"Would a man who speaks with a forked tongue come to you openly?" Fargo countered.

Bull Running considered that. "Why do you not want to kill us as most whites do?"

"I have lived with the red man," Fargo said.

Bull Running considered that, too. He motioned and the others made room at the fire, their unease transparent. "Sit with us. I will hear your words."

Fargo showed no fear. To Comanches cowardice was contemptible. He placed his forearms on his legs, his right arm brushing his holster. "I ask you this," he said. "Did your people attack white wagons and take their women?"

Sparrow Hawk snorted in derision. "White women are of no use to us. They cannot cook. They are weak. They never stop complaining. There is only one use for them." He ran a finger across his throat.

"We did not," Bull Running said.

"The whites think you did."

"The whites are fools."

Fargo smiled. "Some are big fools."

Sparrow Hawk said, "Are you a fool, white-eye?" He ignored a sharp look Bull Running gave him.

"I came to you in peace," Fargo said.

"Maybe it is a trick," Sparrow Hawk said. He turned to the others. "Maybe he is the one."

Sudden suspicion flared on their faces save for Bull Running's. Another young warrior put a hand on the hilt of his knife.

"We should make him tell us."

"We can stake him out so he is a long while dying," another said. "We will cut off his ears and his nose and other parts until he admits he is the one."

Without thinking Fargo blurted in English, "What the hell?" He didn't understand any of this. In their tongue he said, "Who do you think I am?"

"You know," Sparrow Hawk said.

"You asked us about them," another threw in.

Fargo looked at Bull Running. To his dismay, the older warrior appeared troubled. "What is it they think I have done?"

"You could be the one who comes in the night. They say he has hair on his face, as you do. They say he wears a red cloth around his neck, as you do."

Fargo's gut tightened. They were staring at him as cats would stare at a mouse. "I have not done what you think I have."

"Of course you would say that," Sparrow Hawk said.

"Where are they?" asked the one with a long nose. "Where did you take them?"

"Who?"

"Kill him," Sparrow Hawk said.

Steel blades gleamed and lances were raised. Fargo threw himself backward and clawed at the Colt. "I do not want to shoot you," he shouted. They weren't listening. The warrior with the long nose stabbed at his leg, and missed. Lunging, the warrior raised his knife to bury it in Fargo's stomach. Fargo shot him. A lance dug into the ground next to his chest. The man holding it hiked it to thrust again. Fargo shot him. Sparrow Hawk had an arrow nocked and was bringing it to his cheek to aim. Fargo shot him. A fourth warrior leaped, his eyes agleam with bloodlust, his knife poised. Fargo shot him in midair.

Four of the five were down.

Bull Running hadn't moved.

Fargo trained the Colt on him but didn't shoot.

Bull Running's eyes were wide in surprise. Between them was a red-rimmed hole leaking more red. A slug had gone through one of the other warriors, struck Bull Running in the face, and burst out the rear of his cranium. He was dead where he sat.

"Damn it," Fargo fumed, reloading. He hadn't wanted this. He hadn't wanted this at all. He started to rise and heard a footstep behind him.

Fargo whirled.

10

"Don't shoot!" Captain Baker cried. "It's only me."

Fargo looked at the bodies.

"I followed you," Baker said. "I heard you ride off and tried to judge by the sound where you had gone, and damn if I wasn't right." He was proud of his accomplishment.

Fargo shoved the Colt into his holster.

Baker looked at the bodies. "Son of a bitch. You killed all five. By yourself, no less. Shot them so fast, it was over before it started."

"Shut the hell up."

Baker recoiled as if Fargo had slapped him. "What's the matter? I saw them go for you. You didn't have a choice."

"Not one more word about them," Fargo warned. He pivoted on a boot heel and strode to the Ovaro and climbed on. He had gone a short distance when Captain Baker rode alongside.

"Don't get mad. But I'd like to understand. I really and truly would."

"It was a waste," Fargo said. "They didn't attack the wagon train. They didn't take the women."

"Why did they attack you, then? Because you're white?"

"Something else," Fargo said.

"What?"

"I don't know yet." Fargo wished that Baker would stop jabbering.

"How did you stay so calm when they jumped you? I would have been scared to death."

"There wasn't time to think," Fargo said.

"I've been in the army ten years now and I've never been in a fight. Chased a few war parties but never came close enough to swap lead and arrows. That's usually how it is with most of us. We go our whole enlistments without seeing combat. Strange, isn't it?"

"Why are you telling me this?"

"I don't know. Maybe so you'll see why I admire the hell out of you."

"You don't know a damn thing about me," Fargo said.

"I know you can kill like a son of a bitch," Captain Baker declared with a grin.

Major Hargrove's detail hadn't gone far. A trooper at the rear was leading two horses with bodies draped over them. The wounded man was barely able to sit his saddle. The major and Corporal Brunk were in the lead and drew rein when Fargo and Captain Baker trotted up.

"Where the hell did you get to?" Hargrove demanded. "I didn't give permission for you to ride off."

"He killed them," Captain Baker said.

"Who killed who?"

"Fargo killed the Comanches. All five. I saw it with my own eyes."

"I'm supposed to believe that? After he practically begged me not to hurt them?"

"I swear, Major," Captain Baker said. "Send some men back. The bodies are still there."

Hargrove locked his gaze on Fargo. "Cat got your tongue? Did you or didn't you?"

"Were you born a jackass or do you work at it?" Fargo said. He jabbed his spurs and brought the Ovaro to a gallop. Captain Baker hollered and lashed his reins but the Ovaro left the cavalry mount in the dust.

Fargo wanted to be on his own, just him and the untamed wilds: the multitude of stars, the yowls of coyotes, the wind on his face. He noted the position of the North Star and bore to the northwest. He was in no particular hurry.

On a windswept rise Fargo drew rein to rest the Ovaro. He had half a mind to head for Dallas and let the colonel and the major search for the missing women on their own. But without his help they stood little chance.

Fargo sighed. There were times when he was too soft-hearted for his own good. He should rein to the east. He could be in Dallas by the end of the week, treating himself to a high old time. Instead, he continued to the northwest.

Along about the middle of the night Fargo spied a large campfire.

A dozing sentry gave a start and nearly dropped his carbine. "Halt! Who goes there?"

"Who do you think?" Fargo said as he rode past. His arrival woke some of the troopers. They grumbled and rolled over and went back to sleep. He was stripping the Ovaro when Colonel Crowley shuffled up, his hat off, yawning and scratching his mostly bald head.

"Where's the rest of the detail?"

"They'll be along." Fargo untied his bedroll and spread out his blankets.

"Captain Baker isn't with you?"

"I came on ahead."

"I gave specific orders. He wasn't to let you out of his sight."

"I don't need a nursemaid."

Colonel Crowley poked at the ground with his foot. "It's not that I don't think you can handle yourself. I can't afford to have anything happen to you." He did more poking. "Miranda is my only child. We've had our differences but I adore her dearly."

Fargo was undoing the cinch.

"You're our best hope of finding her. My men are competent enough but they're not trackers."

"I'll find her for you," Fargo said. "Without Captain Baker glued to my hip."

"You're annoyed. I suppose I shouldn't blame you. But where's the harm in having him watch your back?"

Grabbing hold of the saddle, Fargo swung it off. "I've changed my mind."

"About what? Captain Baker?"

"In the morning I'm going on ahead. I can make better time alone. Bring your men as fast as you can. I'll mark the trail."

"I wish you wouldn't," Colonel Crowley said.

Fargo removed the saddle blanket. "Keep your eyes skinned for Comanches. I had to shoot a few. It's bound to rile the rest."

"You did what?"

"Hargrove and Baker will tell you about it." Fargo sank down on his back with his head on his saddle and the Henry at his side.

"I'd like to hear more if—"

"Talk to them," Fargo said, and rolled onto his side. The colonel stood there a minute and then shuffled away. Fargo closed his eyes. He tried to drift off but his mind was galloping like the Ovaro. When he finally did fall asleep, it seemed as if he'd barely slept five minutes when his eyes opened again. A faint pink blush painted the eastern sky. He sat up.

Another half an hour or so and the troopers would rouse. He looked for sign of Baker and Hargrove but they hadn't arrived yet. Which was just as well. Rising, he saddled the Ovaro.

The fire had been kept blazing all night. A coffeepot was half full, and Fargo helped himself to a cup. The sentries paid him no mind.

Before sunrise he was under way. It might be rash of him to go after the women by his lonesome but Crowley annoyed him and he didn't much like Hargrove. Or maybe it was the twinge of guilt he felt for not going after them sooner. He told himself he had done the right thing by going to the fort first but if the women died, so much for right.

The sky changed from dark to gray and the stars faded away and on he rode.

"Here I come, ladies," Fargo said.

11

Fargo rode under a blazing sun. The tracks of the twenty and their captives were still plain enough. So long as it didn't rain—and at that time of year it was unlikely—he wouldn't lose their trail.

The wild things, for the most part, shunned the heat. A hawk wheeled in the pale sky. Every so often he saw a rabbit or a deer. Once a rattlesnake slithered across his path.

Water wasn't easy to come by. Most of the streams were dry at this time of year. Others were trickles but trickles were enough when the alternative was to die of thirst.

Then Fargo came on a body. The buzzards and other scavengers had been at it so there wasn't much left. The dress was in tatters but there was enough of it, plus the long blond hair, to tell him it had been a woman. She had been shot in the back of the head. Before she was shot her wrist had been broken and a knee shattered. Someone had hurt her, and hurt her bad.

Fargo picked up his pace. At night, hunched by his fire, the countryside alive with the cries of coyotes, he told himself that he had done the right thing in going to the fort. It pricked at him anyway.

On he rode.

Fargo was aware that a lot of folks back east had the notion that Texas was flat and empty. They were wrong. It had rolling hills and broken country. It had parts so wild, sane men avoided them.

Soon serrated bluffs rose like tombstones. Washes crisscrossed among them. Trees were few but there was mesquite and brush and on the third day, buildings were where there shouldn't be any. One was a lean-to and another a poorly constructed cabin, another slapped together of mismatched boards. The biggest, a saloon, had no door and no glass in the windows. The place looked dead but the three horses tied in front proved otherwise.

Fargo drew rein on a hillock and watched for a spell. No one came out or was moving about. It could be they were staying out of the sun. It could be they had a lookout and had spotted him and were lying in ambush. He gigged the Ovaro, his right hand on his Colt.

A sound from the lean-to made him think of seeds in a dry gourd. It was an old man in rags with an unkempt beard, snoring with his mouth agape. Those of his teeth that weren't missing were yellow. Piled around and under him were torn packs and clothes and empty bottles and a few rusted tools. A skinny mongrel was nosing about.

A woman stood in the cabin doorway. Her dress not much more than a sack, she had a dirty child on her hip. Both stared at him with wary eyes. As he went past she melted into the shadows.

The hitch rail was a sapling. Fargo tied off the reins, shucked the Henry and cradled it, and went into the saloon. The familiar odor of liquor was eclipsed by other foul reeks. He stopped to let his eyes adjust. Dust motes hung like so many gnats. Or maybe they were gnats.

Three men occupied a corner table. The bartender had a beard down to a belly as big around as a washtub. His lizard eyes were lit with false warmth.

"What will it be, friend?"

Fargo stood so he could see the corner table and set the Henry on the plank that served as a bar. "Whiskey."

The man reached under the plank and brought out a half-empty bottle. He produced a glass that had seen a lot of use and poured. "We don't see many strangers in these parts."

"Surprised you see anyone," Fargo said.

The man's burp of a laugh was as genuine as the rest of him. "We're off the beaten path, that's for sure. But we like it that way."

"We sure do," said one of the men at the corner table.

"This flyspeck have a name?" Fargo asked.

"I don't reckon anyone has gotten around to giving it one yet," the barman said, and shrugged. "What's it need one for, anyhow?"

Fargo took a sip. He thought it would be watered down but it wasn't.

"No law says a place has to have a name," the bartender said.

A bulbous fly was crawling on a moldy piece of cheese. On a dirty plate were several chicken bones.

"Not much of a talker, are you?"

Fargo drained the glass and set it down. "Might as well get to it."

"Get to what?" the man asked.

"Twenty riders came through here with four women"—Fargo caught himself—"with three women, less than a week ago. What can you tell me about them?"

The bartender's thick neck went rigid. The men in the corner had been talking in low tones but stopped. The green fly buzzed into the air and settled back on the cheese.

"Nice weather we're having," Fargo said.

48

Chairs scraped, and the three men rose. Hats, clothes, bodies, none had been washed since soap was invented. One had a patch over an eye and a scar under the patch. He also wore a Remington butt-forward on his left hip and his hand was resting on it. The three separated. One moved toward the door, the other took a spot at the end of the bar, while Patch came up to Fargo and smiled. His teeth were worse than the old man's in the lean-to.

"What was that you just said, mister?"

"Nice weather we're having."

Patch blinked his only eye. "No. Not that. Before the weather."

"The twenty riders and the three women."

Patch nodded. "Yeah. That part. What makes you think they came through here?"

"Their tracks come up to the hitch rail," Fargo said. He was watching the one by the door and the one at the end of the bar.

"You looking for them or something?"

Fargo was patient with him. He would get what answers he could before the gunplay. "Would I have asked if I wasn't?"

"Why are you looking?"

"What happened to your eye?"

Patch touched a finger to the circle of rawhide. "What the hell you want to know about this for?"

"Curious," Fargo said.

"I lost it in a knife fight in Galveston. Man said I was cheating at cards and when I pulled my knife he pulled his."

"Were you?"

"Was I what?"

"Cheating."

"Hell no," Patch said. He shifted his weight and his hand

slid lower on the Remington. "Forget about me. We want to know about you. How come you're looking for the riders you say were here?"

"They take things that don't belong to them."

"What did they take?"

"Women."

Patch's scar twitched. He glanced at his friends and at the bartender and said, "You a tin star?"

"You see one pinned on me?"

"Then how come you're nosing around?"

"I have nothing better to do."

Patch's scar did more twitching. "You don't make much sense. Suppose you just come out with it before me and my pards blow holes in you."

"You're welcome to try," Fargo said.

12

His easygoing manner confused them. They were used to scaring folks and he didn't scare. Patch took a step back and the one at the end of the bar took a few steps nearer. The man by the doorway stayed where he was.

"You talk big, don't you?" Patch said.

"You were with them, weren't you?" Fargo answered with a question of his own.

Patch seemed to have a problem holding two thoughts at once. "With who?"

"The men who attacked the wagon train. The men who took the four women and killed one."

A wary gleam came into Patch's remaining eye. "You're poking your nose where you shouldn't ought to."

"You made a mistake, too," Fargo said.

"I don't make mistakes."

"You did if you took the colonel's daughter."

Confusion made Patch's scar twitch nonstop. "What the hell are you talking about now?"

"One of the women was the daughter of the commanding officer at Fort Lancaster. He and a detachment of soldiers aren't far behind me."

"Oh, hell," the bartender said. "Rooster ain't going to like that one bit."

"Shut up, Luis," Patch snapped. He licked his thin lips. "You expect me to believe that?"

Fargo shrugged. "Believe whatever you want. Not that it matters. You won't be here when the colonel shows up."

"I won't? Why?"

"Because you're going to take me to the three women," Fargo said.

"Like hell I am." Patch glanced at the man by the door and the other. "Which one of you wants to do it?"

"Why not all three?" said the man at the end of the bar, and went for his six-gun.

Fargo drew and shot him in the head. Swiveling, he fanned two shots into the man by the door, then jammed the Colt against Patch's scar as Patch was clearing leather. Patch pretended he was a statue.

"So much as twitch," Fargo warned.

"I won't."

Luis was gaping at the crumpled bodies. "God in heaven. I never saw anyone so fast."

Fargo snatched the Remington from Patch's holster and flung it across the room. It skittered across the top of a table and crashed to the floor. "Face the bar."

Patch obeyed.

"Hands out from your side."

Again Patch did as he was told.

Fargo pointed the Colt at the bartender. "Your turn."

"Hold on now!" Luis cried. "I'm not heeled. You can't go shooting me."

"Come over the bar, not around it," Fargo commanded. "Keep your hands where I can see them."

"Sure, sure, whatever you say." Luis hiked his leg onto the plank and slid his foot up and over. He was heavy and ungainly and nearly fell.

"Now then," Fargo said, stepping back. "Tell me about Rooster."

"Who?" Patch said.

Fargo shot him in the leg. Patch shrieked and collapsed. Blood sprayed, and he clamped a hand and cursed.

"Rooster have a last name?" Fargo said to Luis, who gawked in horror at the spreading scarlet. He thumbed back the Colt's hammer.

Luis jerked. "No! No! I'll tell you everything I know. His name is Tremaine. Rooster Tremaine."

"Good," Fargo said.

The old man from the lean-to came through the door with a shotgun. He leveled his cannon, hollered, "I've got him, boys!" and let loose.

Fargo dived even as the saloon rocked to the thunder. He felt a sting in his shoulder and saw Luis's head explode. His hurt shoulder hit the dirt floor and he rolled and fired as the old man brought the shotgun to bear on him, fired as the old man sought to raise it, fired a last shot as the old man crumpled and died with his yellow teeth bared.

Luis's headless body had fallen on top of Patch, who was lying still.

Fargo pushed onto his knees and quickly reloaded. He shoved Luis aside and said, "I'm still waiting to hear about Rooster." He would have to wait longer. Buckshot had caught Patch in the neck and made a ruin of his throat. His mouth was opening and closing but no sounds came out. Patch looked at Fargo, gurgled, and died.

"Damn," Fargo said. He went to the doorway. No one was rushing to see what the ruckus was about.

Fargo went behind the plank. He set the Colt down and pried at his buckskin shirt. Under his sleeve his skin was sticky with blood. He got his arm out but it took a lot of tugging. He was lucky. The flesh was broken but not deep.

Gritting his teeth against the sting, he poured whiskey over the wound. He was pulling his shirt back on when the scrape of a sole brought him around with the Colt in his hand.

The woman had the child on her hip and a knife in her other hand. She was staring at the stump of Luis's neck. "You done killed him."

"Not me," Fargo said, and flicked a finger at the old bundle of rags and filth. "Him."

The woman showed no emotion. "Floyd never could shoot worth a damn."

"What can you tell me about a man called Rooster?"

Shaking her head, the woman backed past him toward a hall at the rear. "He ain't no man. He's the devil."

"Where do I find him?"

"You never do if you want to go on breathing." She stopped, her face in shadow. "I'm lighting a shuck before he comes. You'd be wise to make yourself scarce too."

"Tell me *something*," Fargo said. "I'm trying to find the women he took."

"You never will," she said.

"What makes you say that?"

"No one ever found me."

13

Fargo hurried to the hall. The other end was awash in sunlight. He glimpsed the woman and the child. She was moving fast. He ran to the other end in time to see her dart into the cabin. He crossed and stopped shy of the entrance. It wouldn't do to go bursting in without knowing who was in there besides her and the child.

"Ma'am?"

From the dark bowels came, "Go away."

"I'd like to talk."

"They could show up anytime. I'm getting out while the getting is good."

Fargo heard movement, a scrape and rustling and what might have been a drawer being opened. "What was that about no one found you?"

"Leave me be."

"What can you tell me about Rooster?"

"You are awful pigheaded."

"It's important. A wagon train was attacked. Everyone was killed except for four women."

"That's how Rooster does it," the woman said. "He has other ways, too."

"Does what?"

The door framed her pale figure, the child attached to her

hip as always. "Are you dumb? Haven't you figured it out yet?"

"I'm trying," Fargo said.

"They don't call him the Quiff Man for nothing. It's what he does. He goes around collecting females and then he sells them."

"For sex?"

The woman swiped at a bang. "You don't know nothing. Luis bought me for more than that. A lot of them do."

"*Bought* you?"

"God, I am tired of your stupidity. Rooster finds females. Finds them anywhere and everywhere. Then he sells them to anyone and everyone who wants them." She nodded toward the saloon. "Luis bought me for two hundred dollars five years ago. I'd have fetched more if I was prettier. Although then I was prettier than I am now."

The enormity began to sink in. "Five years? How long has Tremaine been at this?"

"Ten or more years, I reckon."

"And he hasn't been caught?"

"He's mighty slick, the Quiff Man. Gets them from all over. Along the gulf. South of the border. Even from the Indians. Steals them and sells them like he done me."

"How is it the law hasn't heard?"

"What law?" The woman gestured. "You see any law hereabouts? You seen any law for the past month? We are at the godforsaken hind end of the world. There is us and the snakes and scorpions and the Indians and that's all." She started to turn.

"Wait," Fargo said, and moved closer. "I want to put a stop to it."

"You can't."

"Where do I find him?"

"You don't."

"If I wait around will he come back?"

"In six months maybe," the woman said. "He isn't tied to any one place." She paused. "Rooster is a tumbleweed. He goes where the wind takes him."

"Where do you think the wind took him from here?"

"Hell, I hope." She started to back from the door but stopped. "Look. Five years ago I'd have been giddy to have you save me. My folks and I were on our way to San Antonio when Rooster and his men jumped us. They killed my ma and my pa and threw a rope around my neck. I was sixteen."

Fargo did the addition in his head. His surprise must have shown.

"That's right. I'm only twenty-one. Don't look it, do I? I look more like I'm thirty." The child mewed and she bounced it on her hip. "I had hope for a little while that someone would come. But the weeks turned into months and the months into years and I just didn't care anymore. I realized there is no hope in this world. None at all."

"There is now," Fargo said.

She gazed at her dismal surroundings and bowed her head. "Five years too late."

"If you help me I'll take you anywhere you want to go," Fargo offered.

"I can go anywhere anyhow."

"You're in the middle of Comanche country."

"They leave us be because Luis sold them guns," the woman said. "But if they'd known what I know—"

"Think it over," Fargo said. "I'm leaving in half an hour and you're welcome to tag along."

"It could get me killed."

"I'd protect you."

"Hell."

"Think of all the other women who have been through what you have," Fargo said, trying another angle. "Think of all the ones who will suffer if Rooster isn't stopped."

"Hell," she said again, and the cabin's gloom swallowed her.

Fargo went into the saloon. Flies were buzzing around the bodies. A big green one, maybe the same fly that had been on the cheese, was crawling up and over and around the bloody stump of Luis's neck.

He took a bottle and sat at a table and regarded the dead men. Unlike with the Comanches the other night, he had no regrets. Based on what the woman had told him, they'd gotten what they deserved.

Fargo took a long swig and thought about what she'd said.

Slavers were doing a lot of business along the frontier. Slaves were brought in through the bayou country and sold on the auction block for profit. There was a market for indentured servants, too, poor souls who signed their lives away to pay off impossible debts.

This was a new one, though—an illicit trade in women. Fargo wondered who the buyers were. The woman claimed there was more to it than sex. Lonely men, then, desperate for wives? That wasn't so far-fetched. The ratio of males to females was on the order of ten on one. Women were at a premium.

Someone coughed.

Fargo looked up. She had come down the back hall, the child half-asleep, her bangs over her eyes.

"My name is Sarabell."

14

The boy's name was Billybob and he was four years old. As Sarabell explained, her family was from Tennessee. As far back as she could recollect everyone in her family had two first names run together. "To show we're different from everybody else," was how she explained it.

They had been riding since dawn. The sun was almost overhead, the heat of the day withering. Sarabell's pitiful excuse for a dress was wet with sweat and her hair drooped lifeless around her neck. Billybob dozed on her hip.

At least she rode well, Fargo reflected as he tugged on the lead rope to the packhorse. He'd brought supplies for her sake, and for the boy's.

Billybob hadn't uttered a peep. He stared at the world through his large dull eyes, and drooled. Fargo hesitated to ask if anything was the matter with him. It might offend her.

Sarabell wasn't much of a talker, either. She answered questions with as few words as possible and asked none of her own.

Fargo caught her studying him a lot when she thought he wasn't looking.

Toward evening they spooked grouse. Fargo dropped one on the wing with a snap shot from the hip. Pure reflex on his part—and endless hours of practice.

"That was some shooting, mister," Sarabell praised his

skill, and swung down. "Let me fetch it for you." Clutching Billybob, she searched the brush until, with a happy yip, she held the dead bird over her head. "Here it is!"

"We might as well make camp," Fargo proposed. It was early yet but she showed signs of being tired, and then there was the boy.

"You let me do the cooking, you hear?" Sarabell set about collecting firewood and tinder and kindling a flame, all with Billybob in her arm.

Fargo filled his coffeepot from their waterskin and opened his saddlebags for the coffee. He caught her studying him again. "Do I have a wart on my nose?"

"What?" Sarabell laughed. "Goodness gracious, no. You're about the handsomest man I ever did see."

"You're young yet," Fargo said.

Her face clouded. "I don't feel young. I feel a hundred and ten." She hefted Billybob. "Being took, and Luis, made me old before my time."

"You cleaned up nice."

"I did?" She smiled and ran her fingers through her hair. "All I did was wash in the trough. I ain't had me a bath since before I was took. Not that I didn't want one. But Luis said it was a waste of water."

"Nice man, your Luis," Fargo said without thinking.

"He wasn't mine," Sarabell said almost fiercely. "I had my druthers, I'd never have let him touch me. But he bought me, and when I said no, he beat me."

"His beating days are over."

"Thanks to you." Sarabell grinned. "Didn't he look a sight without his head?"

"Doubt he ever used it much," Fargo said.

"Wish I'd of seen it," Sarabell said. "I should've done

it my own self a long time ago except I was too scared of Rooster."

"Why?"

"Because of the—what did Rooster call it?—the guarantee."

"You've lost me," Fargo admitted.

"It's part of Rooster's service, as he calls it. You buy a woman from him, he guarantees she'll make you happy or you get half your money back."

"Only half?"

Sarabell nodded. "Not only that, a woman gives a man trouble, the man can send for Rooster and Rooster will come and knock her around to make her behave." She stopped and her throat rippled. "Rooster or that spooky one."

"Who?"

"They call him Tate. Luther Tate. He's as vicious as can be and he's not afraid of anything. He's the one steals the Injun women."

Fargo stopped pouring coffee. "Does he wear buckskins and a bandanna like me?"

"Matter of fact, he does," Sarabell said, "but he ain't anything like you. He's bone and sinew and has eyes like"—she searched for the right way to say it—"he has eyes like a mad dog."

"I can't wait to meet him," Fargo said.

"Yes, you can." Sarabell commenced plucking the grouse. "He's one of a kind. The only white man alive who will sneak into an Injun village, steal a woman, and waltz out as carefree as you please."

"Comanche women?"

"All kinds."

"Why does he risk losing his scalp?"

"For Rooster. And for the money. There's some as will pay five times what a white girl is worth for a red one. Double that for a Comanche."

"Comanche women will slit the throat of anyone who takes them captive."

"Not if it's done smart. They don't get the chance."

Sarabell fiddled with Billybob's dirty shirt. "Luis told me about a rich man across the border. He has one of those haciendas, and in one of his rooms he keeps two Comanche girls chained to a wall and does with them as he pleases. He paid Rooster a thousand dollars for each. And he's just one of many."

"Someone should get word to the Mexican government," Fargo said.

"It wouldn't do any good. Rooster pays a lot of people to look the other way. He likes to brag he has all sorts of rich and powerful folks in his back pocket."

"We find him, we can end this."

"We?" Sarabell said. "I ain't no good with a gun. And you're just one man. What in hell do you expect to do against Rooster and his whole gang?"

Fargo patted his Colt and said, "What I can."

"It seems to me you're forgetting something."

"What?"

"That bullet business works both ways."

15

Did Sarabell see the three women Rooster took from the wagon train? Yes, she did. But only briefly. She'd been lying on her blanket on the dirt floor of the cabin—

"Blanket?" Fargo interrupted. "You didn't have a bed?"

"Luis wouldn't let me. Said they were a waste of money."

"What the hell did he sleep on?"

"Me."

"I'm happy he's dead," Fargo said.

Sarabell went on. "I heard a whole lot of horses and got up and peeked out. Rooster and Tate and some of the others went into the saloon. The three girls were tied to a rope and were on the ground, worn to a frazzle. I heard a couple of them crying." She bit her lower lip. "It reminded me of me when I was took. I felt real sorry for them."

"You're a good woman."

Sarabell smiled. "I don't know as I'm that but I did try to take them some water in a jug. That awful Tate feller came out and told me to scat or he'd gut me." She bent to the grouse and the feathers.

It would make the plucking easier if she soaked the bird first but they didn't have anything to soak it in so Fargo didn't say anything. He put the coffee on and got his pemmican out and offered a piece to the boy.

"To tide him over."

Billybob stared at it with the same blank emptiness he did everything else.

"Something wrong with him?" Fargo finally mustered the gumption to ask.

Sarabell let out a long breath. She had feathers on her arms and on her chest and in her hair and a few small ones were on her nose. "He's been this way since the time Luis hit him with a stick."

Deep inside of Fargo, something shattered. "Tell me," he said.

She plucked some more before saying, "Billybob was about two, I think it was. He was always a fun baby. Smiled and laughed a lot. The only happiness I had in my life." She wrenched hard on a handful of feathers. "Then one night Luis came home drunk. Billybob had a stomach upset and was crying and when he wouldn't stop, Luis got hold of a big stick and beat him on the head." She gazed at her son. "Ever since, he's been thataway. He just stares. Doesn't laugh or smile or say anything."

"I'm sorry," Fargo said.

"Makes two of us."

There wasn't a feather on the whole bird when Sarabell was done. She slid an old knife with a cracked handle and rust on the blade from her pack and cut the bird's belly so most of the innards spilled out. As she cut she hummed.

"You must like cooking," Fargo said.

"It's not that." She pried the slit wider. "I'm happy, is all. It's been so long, I plumb forgot how good it feels."

"I won't let anything happen to you or your boy," Fargo vowed.

Sarabell brushed at a bang and got gore on her forehead.

"That's mighty sweet. But I know better. This life ain't nothing like I thought it was before they took me."

"It's not all bad."

"It ain't all good, neither. Those that think it is have blinders on." Sarabell held up the heart. "Lookee here. Do you want it or can I? I've always been partial to hearts. They're right tasty."

"It's yours."

"Dang. Me and my boy are free and we're going to eat prairie chicken. Life doesn't get no better than this."

Sarabell roasted the grouse to a turn. She'd brought half a loaf of moldy bread from her cabin and a handful of scrawny potatoes. Fargo declined the bread but accepted slices of potato after she cooked them.

"Too bad we don't have butter."

"Luis didn't much care for it," Sarabell said. "I begged him for a cow but he'd always slap me and tell me to hush."

Night spread its indigo mantle. As usual, coyotes were abroad. So was a fox that came close, drawn by the aroma of the meat. It stood there so long that finally Fargo threw a stone to drive it away.

Billybob had to be hand-fed. Each mouthful was a challenge. Sarabell coaxed him into opening wide and then spooned the food in before he closed it.

"Is this how you always feed him?"

"Have to," Sarabell said. "He won't eat a lick otherwise. Inside of a week he'd starve."

"You care for him a lot."

"That's plain silly. He's my son. Of course I do." She hugged the boy and kissed his cheek. "He's my treasure. Without him I'd have blown my brains out years ago."

"You're a good mother."

"I do what comes natural."

They sat and sipped hot black coffee while above them a shooting star cleaved the heavens.

"I thank you for this," Sarabell said softly. "I could die in a minute and go content. I never thought I'd be my own woman again."

"When we catch up to Rooster, hang back so he doesn't know you're with me."

Sarabell reached over and placed her hand on his knee. "I wish you'd listen to me. You say the army is after him? Let the army deal with him, then."

"I don't know how far back they are," Fargo said. Or even if they were still following him. For all of Colonel Crowley's bluster about wanting revenge, Crowley might have turned around and gone back to the fort.

"It can't all be on you," Sarabell said, and hesitated. "I like you, mister. You've done me right and I don't want you hurt."

"I'm obliged."

"But you're going on anyway?"

"I have it to do."

Sarabell sulked. Fargo tried to cheer her but she was a clam. She and the boy turned in early and he sat by the fire thinking about those who kidnapped and sold women and beat babies with sticks.

16

The Gonzales brothers were horse thieves. They crossed into Mexico and stole horses and brought them back and sold them on the Texas side of the border or they stole horses from Texas ranchers and drove the animals into Mexico and sold them there.

Fargo had heard of them. He hadn't heard of their haven deep in the wilds, a collection of cabins and shacks that ringed a large corral filled with horses. Flat on his belly at the edge of a bluff, he tried to count the people moving about and drinking and relaxing and stopped at thirty-two.

"There are too many," Sarabell said. "We should turn tail."

"Do you see the three women?"

Sarabell suddenly stiffened. "No. But I see *him*. Rooster and his men are here, all right. I told you he'd come here next."

"Which one is Rooster?"

"See the big man by the oak tree? The fancy pants?"

It was a good description. Rooster Tremaine was tall and well built and dressed in fine clothes. From his white hat down to his polished boots, he looked as out of place as fine china in an outhouse. At the moment he was talking to half a dozen men stamped from the same mold as Patch and his friends.

"The girls must be inside," Sarabell guessed. "Getting them out won't be easy."

A lanky man stepped from under the oak tree.

"See that one? It's Luther Tate." Sarabell gripped Fargo's arm. "The mean one."

From that distance it was hard to be sure but Tate looked to be about Fargo's size and wore buckskins and a bandanna and had a beard.

"No wonder the Comanches mistook me for him."

"What's your plan?" Sarabell asked.

"I haven't come up with one yet."

"For your own sake I hope it doesn't get you killed."

Fargo slid away from the edge and stood. He stepped to the packhorse and took down the waterskin. "You and the boy should have some."

Sarabell came over. Before Fargo could guess her intent, she shoved Billybob at him. He put an arm around the boy's waist and Sarabell took the waterskin.

"Hold him for me."

The boy didn't squirm or fidget, just looked at Fargo with those dull eyes. Fargo shivered even though it was hot as hell.

Sarabell carefully let the water trickle down her son's throat. Billybob didn't smile or smack his lips or anything. "There you go," she said when she gauged he'd had enough.

They swapped, and Fargo hung the waterskin on the packhorse. He was getting to like this feisty woman. It took a lot of grit to endure what she had.

"Why are you looking at me like that?"

"Just thinking about how tough you are."

"Me?" Sarabell laughed. "Mister, you have me mistook with somebody else. I'm so tough I let a man keep me like an animal for five years."

"What else could you have done?"

"If I was as tough as you think, I'd have stuck a knife in him while he was sleeping and run off."

"With Comanches and outlaws everywhere, and you with a baby."

"Quit making excuses for me. I'm not tough and don't ever think I am. I just do what I have to do to go on living."

Sarabell walked off, practically stabbing the ground with every step.

Fargo was puzzled. Here he thought he'd given her a compliment. He went near the edge, flattened, took off his hat, and poked his head over. Nothing had changed. Rooster was still by the oak tree. A pair of stocky men in sombreros, the Gonzales brothers he reckoned, were drinking and laughing with a bunch of others at the corral. He didn't see Luther Tate.

Fargo had been watching about half an hour when Rooster Tremaine went into a shack and reappeared, leading three young women by a rope. Sarabell had mentioned that when she saw the women they were worn to exhaustion. Apparently Rooster had let them rest and made them spruce up.

Fargo could read the fear in their faces, and in their bearing. They were terrified.

Rooster made for the corral. Luther Tate and several others flanked him. Fargo noticed that those in Tate's path were quick to get out of the way.

The Gonzales brothers were in good spirits. They laughed and clapped Rooster on the arm and then they went from woman to woman, touching and squeezing and pulling on their hair. One of the brothers cupped a breast and the woman tried to kick him. Both brothers thought that was hilarious.

Not Rooster. He was on the woman before she realized it. A blow to her face knocked her down. A boot to her stomach doubled her over. The Gonzales who had grabbed her breast went to intervene and stopped cold when Luther Tate materialized at Rooster's side.

The woman was crying. The other two sought to comfort her but Rooster jerked on the rope and cuffed them. They cowered before his brutality but he went on hitting them.

Rooster wasn't done. He stepped to the woman on the ground, bent, and seized the front of her dress. She slapped at his arm and he punched her. With a violent wrench, he ripped her dress open to the waist. She tried to cover herself and he seized her by the hair and shook her.

The Gonzales brothers and Rooster talked. The brothers did a lot of gesturing and Rooster shook his head a lot. Haggling, Fargo guessed. Finally Rooster nodded and one of the brothers went to the woman on the ground, cut the rope around her wrists, and hauled her to her feet. She held her dress in front of her and wouldn't look at him.

A foot crunched on the dirt next to Fargo and Sarabell eased down. "Learned anything?"

"There are a lot of bastards in this world."

"Hell," Sarabell said. "I could have told you that."

17

Nature seemed to be on Fargo's side.

Toward evening the wind began to gust and dark clouds swept out of the west. By the time night fell, clouds covered much of the sky. It was so dark Fargo could barely see his hand at arm's length. He was sharpening the toothpick on a whetstone when Sarabell broke a long silence.

"You're fixing to sneak on down there, aren't you?"

"You saw the three women," Fargo said.

"What are they to you? You don't even know them."

"I didn't know you." Fargo ran the edge of the toothpick across his thumb and a tiny red line welled up. He began honing the other edge.

"Is this what you do? Go around rescuing folks?"

"What I try to do is mind my own damn business. Now and then I can't."

"Can't or won't?"

Fargo looked up. "There are some things a man can't abide and still call himself a man."

"Such as?"

"I won't be laid a hand on. The things I don't do to people, I don't let anyone do to me."

"Rooster and his men never laid a hand on you or insulted you."

"You're forgetting Patch and his friends."

Sarabell frowned. "I just don't want anything to happen to you. You're the only damn friend I've got."

"I'll be careful," Fargo promised.

"That doesn't count for much. Life doesn't always do what we want it to do."

"I'm going," Fargo said.

Sarabell gazed toward the corral. "I wish you wouldn't but I know you will. I take it I'm to stay with the horses?"

"Best for you and the boy." Fargo tested the other edge. He slid the toothpick into his ankle sheath, lowered his pant leg, and patted it.

"What do I do if you don't come back?"

"Get on the horses and ride like hell for Fort Lancaster. With any luck you'll run into Colonel Crowley and his men."

"That officer you've told me about?" Sarabell nodded. "Are you sure he's even still following you?"

"No."

Fargo left the Henry in the saddle scabbard. In the dark the Colt would do as well. He moved to the trail that would take him to the bottom. He had studied it before the sun went down and memorized every turn. He was about to start down when her hand fell on his shoulder. "I can't hold off any longer."

"I know." Sarabell's face was pale in the night. She nervously smiled, then rose onto her toes and kissed him on the cheek. "For luck."

"Take care of yourself, Sarabell Lee."

"You too."

Fargo's big worry was that stones and dirt would slide from under his feet and give him away. He went slow, testing each step before he applied his weight. Campfires were burning but none were near enough to the bluff for their light to give him away.

The women-stealers and the rustlers were having a grand time. Bottles were passed around. Men joked and laughed. Some were gambling. Others were fondling women. The three Rooster Tremaine had brought weren't the only females. The rustlers had a few of their own.

Fargo hadn't seen Rooster or Luther Tate in a while. Two of the woman had been taken back into a shack while the third, the one the Gonzales brother picked, had been pushed into a cabin and the door slammed after her.

Fargo was surprised there were no guards. This was Comanche country, after all. Maybe the brothers gave the Comanches horses and in return the Comanches let them go on breathing. Comanches were great admirers of good horseflesh.

Fargo reached the bottom and crouched. He was close enough now that he could hear a welter of voices.

". . . pass that bottle . . ."

". . . a whore who only had one ear. She got it cut off in a fight with another whore who . . ."

". . . gruella is a damn fine animal. We should get good money for . . ."

Fargo circled. There was plenty of cover. He came up on the cabin from the rear and rose in its shadow. There was no window. He glided around to the side. Again, no window. The Colt in his hand, he moved to the front. Firelight splashed over the closed door. To reach it he must show himself.

Several men in sombreros were approaching. They passed a bottle back and forth. The man in the middle was a Gonzales brother, the same brother who had picked the woman earlier. They stopped and Gonzales tilted the bottle and took a long swallow.

"Drink it all, amigo," a man said.

"Or maybe save some for the *chica*," another suggested. "To make her more willing, eh?"

The Gonzales brother lowered the bottle and wiped his mouth with his sleeve. "Willing or not, I will make her mine. I have paid a lot of money."

"Do you think Rooster told you the truth?"

"That she is the daughter of the coronel at Fort Lancaster? *Sí*."

Fargo hadn't known which of the three was Miranda Crowley. Now he did.

"Rooster is not to be trusted in some things but he would not lie about this."

"He is a strange one."

"Luther Tate is stranger."

"Enough," the Gonzales brother said. He sucked down the rest of the bottle and tossed it to the ground. "My new wife awaits." He hitched at his pants, inserted a key in the door, and strode inside.

18

Fargo raised the Colt. The other two chuckled and walked toward the fire. The moment their backs were turned, Fargo slipped around the corner. He put his ear to the door. Gonzales's voice, although muffled and slurred by drink, was clear enough.

"Put that down. You do not want to make me mad."

Miranda Crowley's voice was defiant. "I will by God bash your brains out if you try to have your way with me."

Gonzales laughed. "Do you want me to send for Rooster? He gave me his word you would do as I want, and he doesn't like it when a woman makes a liar of him."

"I don't care what you do, bean-eater."

"That bruise on your face didn't teach you anything, did it, you stupid gringo bitch?" Gonzales wasn't in a good mood anymore. "But you are right. You are mine, not his. I will teach you to obey me."

There was a sharp cry and the sounds of a scuffle.

Fargo opened the door, slipped in, and closed the door behind him. The cabin had only one room. To the left was a narrow bed with rumpled blankets, to the right a table and a chair. Directly across, Miranda Crowley had her back to the wall and was flailing at the Gonzales brother with, of all things, a chamber pot. His sombrero was at his feet. Gonzales blocked a blow and clamped his other hand on her throat.

"Drop it, *puta*. I will not warn you again."

Fargo was behind him before either realized he was there. He slashed the Colt down, once, twice, three times, and Gonzales's thick legs buckled and he keeled onto his side with blood trickling from the back of his head and his fingers twitching.

Miranda Crowley's green eyes flashed with fury. She had tied her torn dress together with twine so it covered most of her bosom. "You won't defile me, either, you damn cutthroat."

"Your father sent me," Fargo said.

"A likely story. You just don't want me to brain you."

"Your father and Major Hargrove and about forty troopers are a few days behind me," Fargo explained. "We have to get you out of here."

Miranda lowered the chamber pot part way. "Damn me if you don't sound sincere."

Fargo held out his hand to her. "We don't have time to waste."

"Hold on," she said. "After the hell I've been through, how can I trust you?"

"Your father told me once that the thing he does best in life is eat." Fargo motioned at Gonzales. "If I was one of their men, would I know that?"

Miranda let the chamber pot drop even lower. "You might have seen my father somewhere. One look, and it's obvious he likes his food."

"Damn it, girl," Fargo said. He racked his brain. "How about this? Your father once saw a friend of his killed by Apaches and hasn't been the same since."

"Oh God. You know about that?" Miranda lowered the chamber pot all the way. "It twisted him inside, made him less than he was."

Fargo offered his hand again. "We have to get the other two."

Miranda set the pot down and took his hand. "Why bother?"

Fargo had started to turn. "What was that?"

"You try to help them, you're likely to be caught," Miranda said. "Where would that leave me?"

"I'm here for all three of you."

"I should come first. I mean, my father *is* an officer, and you're under his command."

Fargo didn't like what he was hearing. "I'm not with the army."

"You're doing this on your own? What kind of idiot are you?"

"Idiot?"

"Don't get me wrong," Miranda said. "I'm grateful. But if it was me, I wouldn't risk my skin to save yours." She smiled sweetly. "Save me and forget about those other two."

"Or I can save them and forget about you."

"You're mad, aren't you? You think I'm coldhearted. But I'm being practical. Take me to safety. Amy and Catherine can escape on their own."

"You'd desert your friends?"

"Friends, hell," Miranda said. "I hardly know them."

Fargo cracked the door open. Over by the corral a man was chugging from a bottle. Somewhere a woman laughed. No one was near the cabin. He opened the door wide enough to slip out. Miranda followed, her fingers cold in his hand. They darted around to the side. Keeping low, they moved in a half-circle. Fargo stopped about ten yards from the shack where the other two women were being held.

"What are you doing?" Miranda Crowley asked.

"I've already told you." Fargo pulled on her arm but she wouldn't budge.

"And I've already told *you*. Get me out and come back for them if you must but get me out first." She tried to tug free. "And let go."

Fargo pulled harder and she stumbled and nearly fell. Hauling her after him, he crept closer. She stopped resisting.

The outlaws were making so much noise that he didn't have to worry about being heard.

They came to the end of the brush.

"Wait here," Fargo said.

"Gladly."

The door was barred. Fargo was lifting it when shapes hove out of the dark.

19

Fargo let the bar down and made it to the side of the shack before they spotted him.

Rooster Tremaine came out of the darkness. Behind him were Luther Tate and others. Rooster raised the bar and leaned it against the shack and opened the door. "Come on out, ladies." He had a fine, deep voice.

"What for?" a woman fearfully asked.

"Because I said to. No need for the two of you to stay cooped up in here when the rest of us are having fun."

The other woman said, "You don't fool us. You intend to get us drunk and have your way with us."

"Stupid bitch," Luther Tate said.

Rooster leaned against the jamb. "Has anyone laid a finger on you since the wagon train?"

"No, but—" the same woman began.

Rooster held up a hand, silencing her. "I told you before, Amy, that—"

"It's Miss Sutter to you."

"—I told you that you're worth more to me pure than you are used."

"Maybe I'm not as pure as you think," Amy said.

"Just so you look healthy and happy when I sell you."

"Happy?" the other woman exploded. "You slaughtered

our loved ones and took us captive and we're supposed to be *happy*?"

"Don't raise your voice to me, Catherine," Rooster Tremaine said. "You saw what I did to Miranda."

"Too bad you didn't shoot her," Amy said.

Rooster stepped back and beckoned and the two women slowly emerged. Tate and the others fell in on either side of them and they were escorted to the corral.

Fargo swore under his breath and hurried into the brush to where he had left Miranda. "There's a hitch."

"I saw. I told you we shouldn't waste our time."

"I'm going to wait for them inside," Fargo said. "You keep watch. If things go as I hope, Rooster will bar the door and leave. As soon as you can, come over and let us out and we'll light a shuck."

"You expect a lot from me."

"Don't start." Fargo returned to the shack. He crawled around to the door and slipped inside. Once he was sure no one could see him, he stood. A lantern hung on a peg. Two shoddy beds with moth-eaten blankets were at opposite walls. On a table were dirty plates and forks and spoons.

Fargo moved to the corner to the left of the door. The only thing to do now was wait.

Over an hour passed. Voices warned him they were coming back, and he crouched and cocked the Colt.

"Get your rest now, ladies. We have a long ride ahead of us tomorrow," Rooster Tremaine was saying.

"Being nice to us won't make us like you better," Amy told him.

"I'm nice until you give me trouble. Now in you go."

"Where are you taking us, anyhow?" Catherine asked. "You haven't said."

"South."

"How far south?" Catherine asked when he didn't elaborate. "The border country? All the way to Mexico?"

"You'll find out when we get there."

The first woman came in and then the second. They were looking back at Rooster Tremaine and didn't notice Fargo. The door closed and the bar scraped.

"At least they haven't raped us," Amy said. She was the smaller of the two. Slender but shapely, she had brunette curls and a nice mouth.

"I wish I could get my hands on a pistol," Catherine said. She was almost as tall as Fargo. She had a high forehead and a full mouth that perpetually pouted.

Their dresses were homespun. Both had the tanned look of farm girls.

"Ladies," Fargo whispered.

Both of them spun. Amy opened her mouth to scream but didn't. Catherine stared at the Colt and said, "Touch us and your boss will have your hide."

Fargo moved to the door. With each step he took, they took a step back. "I'm not here to hurt you."

"Like hell," Catherine said.

"My name is Fargo. Colonel Crowley is on his way from the fort to rescue his pride and joy and I thought we'd rescue you as well."

Hope sprang into Amy's face but Catherine was skeptical. "Why should we believe you?"

"Cathy," Amy said.

"It could be a trick. He lures us out, and him and his friends jump us."

Fargo had an ear to the door. "In a few moments Miranda will lift the bar. Once we're out, stay close."

"You already freed her?" Amy asked.

"From a fate worse than death." Fargo was still listening but heard nothing.

"You say Miranda is out there?" Catherine said. "Why hasn't she released us?"

"Maybe the coast isn't clear."

Amy was rigid with expectation. "Do you hear her yet?"

"No."

"What is she waiting for?" Catherine demanded.

Fargo wished to hell he knew.

20

"I can't believe you trusted her," Catherine McDonald said. "But maybe you don't know what she's like."

A couple of hours had gone by. The bar was still in place. Fargo was hunkered with his back to the door.

"We could have warned you about sweet Miranda," Amy Sutter said. She was perched on a bed, her knees together, her elbows on her legs and her chin in her hands.

"Could we ever," Catherine said. "From the moment I met her I didn't like her."

"She looks down her nose at everybody," Amy said. "That poor man of hers had no notion he was being used."

"Used?" Fargo repeated.

Amy nodded. "She married him to get away from her father. She came right out and told us that as soon as they reached California, she was throwing him over for somebody better."

Fargo closed his eyes and sighed. He had been up since before dawn and here it was well into the night and he was tired and hungry and mad.

"Do you think the army will get here soon?" Amy asked.

"No."

"They take too long, we'll be in Mexico," Catherine said, "and they can't cross the border to come after us." Her eyes misted. "I rue the day my folks decided we should move to Santa Fe."

From outside came a commotion: yells and the pound of hooves and the whinny of a horse. A man bellowed for quiet. It sounded like Rooster Tremaine. Soon Fargo heard voices but he couldn't make out what they were saying. Someone thumped on the door. He jumped to his feet and backed into the corner not a moment too soon. The bar was removed and the door was flung wide.

"Come on out here," Rooster Tremaine said.

Amy and Catherine started to obey.

"Not you two," Rooster snapped. "The hombre who's in here with you."

Both women glanced at the corner and Amy said innocently, "What hombre?"

"Don't make me come in there." Rooster raised his voice. "You hear me, mister?"

"I hear you," Fargo said.

"Holster your hardware and step out with your hands where we can see them. Try anything—anything at all—and we'll put windows in your skull."

Fargo did as they wanted.

A semicircle of rustlers and outlaws bristled with weapons. Some held torches. Behind them was the Ovaro and Sarabell's horse and their pack animal.

Rooster Tremaine and Luther Tate stood next to the Gonzales brothers. Near Tremaine, her head bowed in despair, was Sarabell.

Fargo stood still as Luther Tate relieved him of the Colt. Up close, he could feel the potent force of the killer's cold glare. "Nice to meet you," he quipped.

Tate stepped back and didn't say a word.

"In case you're wondering how we knew you were inside—" Rooster said, and he stepped aside and gestured.

Miranda Crowley's wrists were bound and she had a fresh

bruise on her cheek but she stood with her shoulders squared and her chin high.

"Hell," Fargo said.

"One of my men spotted her slinking off," Rooster Tremaine revealed. "We followed her up the bluff and found Sarabell and the horses."

"I would have gotten away if not for that cow," Miranda said.

Rooster smiled. "It seems she wanted to take your horse and Sarabell wouldn't let her. They were having quite the tussle when we snuck up on them."

"The bitch," Miranda said.

The Gonzales brother Fargo had knocked out swore and said, "She is not the only one, *puta*."

"Go to hell, greaser."

Gonzales balled his fist and moved toward her but stopped and glanced uncertainly at Rooster Tremaine and then at Luther Tate.

"You paid for her. She's yours," Rooster said. "You can beat the hell out of her. Break her legs. Kill her if you want. Up to you."

"He wouldn't dare," Miranda said.

Gonzales grinned and punched her in the stomach. He didn't hold back.

Miranda folded over, her face nearly purple. Gasping and wheezing, she sucked in deep breaths. Incredibly, she smirked at Gonzales and said, "Is that the best you can do, you weak sister?"

"Isn't she something?" Rooster marveled.

Gonzales didn't think so. He clubbed her over the back of her head and she dropped like a poled calf. He raised his boot to stomp on her but his brother pushed him back.

"No, Carlos. Think of what you paid for her."

Carlos reluctantly nodded. "I want my money, Rooster. You always say that if we are not pleased we can have it back."

"Have you fucked her yet?"

"No," Carlos said, and there were laughs and snickers. "I didn't get to."

"Then how do you know she's not worth it?"

"She ran away—"

Rooster cut him off. "She was taken by him." Rooster nodded at Fargo. "He's the one you should be upset at, not me."

The other Gonzales said something in Carlos's ear.

"Tell you what I'll do, though," Rooster said. "You've always been fair when you sold me horses so I'll return the favor." He gripped Miranda's arm and pushed her at Carlos.

"Take her and fuck her and if you still don't want her, I'll take her back and give you almost all of your money."

"Almost?"

"I came a long way to sell her to you," Rooster said. "Ten percent would cover my expenses."

"Always the businessman."

"Do we have a deal?"

Carlos gnashed his teeth and swore. "*Sí*. We have a deal." He pointed at Fargo. "What about the one who hit me?"

"I'll throw him in for free," Rooster said. "Do whatever you want."

Carlos stalked up to Fargo. "Did you hear him, gringo? You are mine." His face split in sadistic glee. "Which would you like to lose first? Your fingers? Your nose? Or maybe your cojones?"

21

Fargo swore he could feel the blood draining into his head. It hurt like hell. His wrists stung. His ankles were sore. The breeze picked up, rustling the leaves of the oak, and he swayed at the end of the rope like a buckskin-clad pendulum.

It was pushing midnight and most of the women-stealers had turned in. Rooster planned to head out early. Some of the rustlers were still by the corral, drinking and talking, but they weren't as rowdy.

The tree limb creaked with each swing. Fargo held himself still hoping the rope would stop. They'd taken his hat and his bandanna. His gun belt and the Colt were also gone.

Amy and Catherine were back in the shack. Carlos Gonzales had dragged Miranda Crowley into the cabin and slammed the door and that was the last anyone heard of them. There were no screams, no wails, no pleading for him to leave her be.

Fargo was fuming. Just about everything that could go wrong had gone wrong. He raised his head to try to lessen some of the pain but it only made his neck hurt more.

A pair of rustlers approached, each with a bottle. They walked as if they were on the pitching deck of a ship. One tilted his sombrero and raised his bottle in a mock salute.

"Hey, gringo. I would not want to be you, eh?"

The other swilled and shook his head. "Me either. I am fond of my cojones."

That brought a lot of snickering.

"Nothing to say, senor?" the first man said.

"Maybe you would like a drink, yes?" said the other.

"I could use a knife," Fargo told them.

They could barely stay on their feet, they laughed so hard.

The first one came directly underneath. "What you will need to do is bite your tongue off when Carlos starts cutting on you. Maybe you will choke to death in your own blood and spare yourself the rest."

The other man nodded. "That is a good idea, Pacho. Better to choke than to lose bits of himself piece by piece."

"I won't have to if you'll give me a knife," Fargo said.

Pacho clapped the other on the back. "This gringo is a funny man."

"*Sí*. When he dies we will drink to him and his tongue."

Off they ambled, singing.

Fargo fought his own impatience. He still had the toothpick in his boot but he needed to wait until all of them turned in.

The constellations crawled across the firmament. The last of the fires dwindled. The few rustlers still up were passing a bottle back and forth.

Fargo couldn't feel his feet. He twisted and turned, seeking to restore his circulation, but it didn't help. His feet tingled a little and that was all.

A figure came out of the dark. Someone in a sombrero and a serape. Whoever it was leaned against the oak and looked up at him, their face in shadow.

"Go away," Fargo said.

A blade flashed and the rope parted, and the next Fargo knew, his shoulders hit the ground and he nearly blacked out. He lay dazed until he felt fingers on his arm, rolling him over. The head under the sombrero bent low.

"Miss me?" Miranda Crowley said.

Fargo glanced toward the fire. No one had seen him drop. "Where's Carlos Gonzales?"

"In hell, I hope." Miranda rolled him onto his side. "Hold still. I don't want to cut your wrists by mistake."

There was a sting and the rope gave way. Fargo went to rub his arms and pain shot up them. "My feet," he said.

Miranda was a black silhouette under the sombrero. "Not so fast. I want your word first."

"My word on what?" Fargo was uneasy lying there in the open.

"Why do you think I cut you down? I learned my lesson earlier. I can't get away on my own. I need your help."

"I'll help you. Now cut my legs free."

"Hold your horses." Miranda put her face inches from his. "That's not what I want your word on."

"Then what, damn it?" Any moment, Fargo worried, someone would spot them.

"I want your word that you'll take me and only me. Not that little bitch Amy or that big bitch Catherine or that hayseed and her kid."

"You'd leave them behind?"

"I told you before and it didn't sink in. They're nothing to me. Amy and Catherine have never liked me. As for the hayseed, I wouldn't be here now if not for her. I was trying to ride off and she stopped me, the bitch."

"You ask too much," Fargo said.

"Either you give your word or I'll give a holler and run," Miranda threatened. "They'll all come to see what the ruckus is about and while they're busy with you I'll try my luck on my own. I don't want to but I will."

Fargo believed her. The only person she truly cared about was herself. "You'll have to help me to the cabin."

"Why?"

"I can hardly move. I need time. We can hide there until I'm back to normal."

"I don't like delaying," Miranda said. But she sliced the rope around his ankles and helped him stand.

Fargo draped an arm across her shoulders and leaned so heavily that her legs almost buckled.

"Damn, you're heavy," Miranda huffed. "Wouldn't think it to look at you."

Thankfully, the cabin wasn't far. Fargo's arms and legs were tingling with torment and Miranda was puffing when they eased through the door and she kicked it shut behind them.

The lantern had burned low. In its yellow glow the red of blood was almost black. Carlos Gonzales lay on his back with his limbs spread-eagle. His sombrero was partially crushed under him. Both of his eyes were wide in surprise, as well they should be—his throat had been slit from ear to ear.

"How did you get hold of his knife?" Fargo asked.

"I let him think I gave in," Miranda said. "I stopped fighting and said if it was going to happen, I might as well enjoy it." She kicked the body. "The pig. He was groping my bottom and I reached around and plucked his knife as easy as you please." She demonstrated, smiling. "He was kissing my ear when I said his name. Do you know what he asked me? 'What do you want, my little beauty?'" Miranda laughed. "One cut was all it took. You should have seen his face."

Fargo took a few steps, forcing his legs to cooperate by force of will. "Give me his revolver." He had no idea where his own had gotten to.

Miranda squatted and slid it from the holster and handed it over. "Here you go."

Fargo was in luck. It was a Colt with pearl grips. The barrel was longer than the barrel on his but it was the same caliber. He made sure it was loaded and wedged it under his belt so that the pearl grips were above the buckle. "Tell me something. Does your father know how you are?"

"I am my own person and he doesn't like me that much. He claims I'm too self-centered for my own good. Can you imagine?"

Yes, Fargo could.

"He expected me to go on living at the fort even though I told him and told him I was tired of army life." Miranda's face took on a dreamy quality. "I want to live in a big city somewhere. San Francisco, maybe. The climate is nice and there are dress shops galore and restaurants and carriages and the theater—" She clasped her hands to the serape. "It would be heaven."

"So you married a farmer?"

Miranda laughed. "He was a means to an end. My father would never have let me go off on my own but he damn certain couldn't stop me if I was someone's wife."

"Does it bother you that your husband is dead?"

"Why should it?"

Fargo tried to move his arms and legs. His legs were still wobbly but his arms were coming along nicely.

"How much longer? We had a deal and I'm holding you to it."

"I never said we did."

"You son of a bitch," Miranda said, and came at him with the knife.

22

Fargo sprang back and nearly fell and the blade whisked past his throat. She thrust at his chest. He sidestepped and twisted and when she lunged at his throat again he grabbed her wrist and wrenched. Miranda cried out and the knife fell at her feet. He pushed her and she tripped and reached for the wall to keep from falling. Bending, he picked up the knife.

Miranda's face was aflame with rage. "After I went and saved you, you do this."

"You did it to save yourself." Fargo went to the door and opened it a few inches and listened. No one had heard her outcry. No one had discovered he was missing yet, either. He closed the door.

"You aim to try and save them, don't you?"

Fargo looked at her.

"Of course you do," Miranda said bitterly. "You have to be noble and heroic and get me killed doing it."

"Noble and heroic, hell."

"What else would you call it?"

"When you see an animal with rabies, you shoot it."

"You're talking about Tremaine? About him and his men?"

"There was a dead baby with the bodies at the wagon train," Fargo said.

"I was there, remember? Luther Taft killed it. Shot it through the head."

"Well now," Fargo said.

"What can I do to make you forget the others and only save me?" Miranda smiled and cupped a breast. "How about if I let you have me? Right here. Right now. Do whatever you want and when you're done we leave. Just the two of us. Not Amy or Catherine or the hayseed."

"Jesus," Fargo said.

"What?"

"Don't talk."

"I will if I want to and there's nothing you can do."

"I can punch you in the mouth."

That shut her up. Fargo did a few deep-knee bends to ensure his legs were working. He opened the door again. Two men were at the fire, drinking. Everyone else had turned in. "We'll wait a while yet."

Miranda sank down and sat with her arms around her legs. "You don't like me very much, do you?"

"About as much as I like pus."

"Because I speak my mind?"

"Because you're a bitch."

The men at the fire rose. One yawned and stretched and the other scratched his crotch. They shambled around the corral and over to where sleeping forms were bundled in blankets. In a little bit they spread out their own and curled on their sides.

"You don't know what it's been like being me," Miranda said gloomily.

"And I don't want to."

"My whole life, I've been dragged all over by my father. From post to post to post. Not the good posts, either. The army always sent him to the most godforsaken spots. Half the time there weren't any kids my own age."

"Is this where I break out in tears?"

"Bastard. I'm trying to explain. To show you I'm the way I am because of the life I've had to live. A tough life. A hard life. With few friends and no relatives anywhere near. Think about that."

Despite himself, Fargo did. "Hard is one thing. Running out on Amy and Catherine—and me—is another."

"I'm not a coward."

"Never said you were. I said you were a bitch."

"Anyone ever call you a son of a bitch?"

"All the time," Fargo said.

"Then I guess we're more alike than you'll admit."

Fargo turned from the door. "We'll do what we can to get them out. Maybe we can't but we have to try."

Miranda smacked the ground. "All right. We'll do it your way. But I don't have to be happy about it. And I'm not taking a bullet for any of them—you hear me?"

"Be careful," Fargo said.

"Of what?"

"You're almost acting human."

Miranda cupped both her breasts. "Are you sure I can't interest you?"

"Bitch fits you like a glove."

Fargo took hold of her wrist and opened the door and slipped out into the cool of the night. The camp was quiet. The horses in the corral were still. He made straight for the shack. Off across the badlands a fox yowled. He skirted a yucca and avoided dry brush that might crackle underfoot.

He was almost to the shack and could see that the bar was in place when a man came around from the other side, carrying a rifle.

23

The guard was looking the other way.

Fargo let go of Miranda and drew the Colt and smashed it above the man's ear.

With a bleat of surprise, the man folded.

Fargo shoved the Colt under his belt. He raised the bar and set it to aside and opened the door. Inside was pitch black. "Sarabell?" he said, and got no answer. "Amy? Catherine?" Still no reply.

"They're not here," Miranda whispered.

"Then why was the door barred?"

A gurgling whine drew Fargo in. He moved slowly, edging forward until he bumped something that moved. Kneeling, he touched a leg. Both ankles were tied. So were both arms. He lightly ran his fingers over the woman's shoulder to her neck and face. A gag was in place. He removed it and the person coughed.

"Thank you," Sarabell said.

"The other two here?"

"Somewhere," Sarabell said. "Billybob, too. Please free me so I can find him."

Fargo drew the toothpick. By feel he pressed an edge to the rope around her wrists and slowly sliced. The toothpick was as sharp as the sharpest razor; he had to be careful not to cut her.

"I'll untie my legs," she said when the last of the strands parted.

Fargo groped to one side and then the other. His fingers slid across another pair of bound legs. This time it was Amy.

"I'm so glad you're alive. I thought you were a goner."

Catherine was a few feet away. She spat and swore and jiggled her arms. "Get me free. We have to get out of here before they catch us."

A soft squeal of delight told Fargo that Sarabell had found Billybob. He moved to the doorway expecting Miranda to be there—but she was gone. "Son of a bitch," he said. His blood froze in his veins when he spotted her in the act of opening the corral. Several horses had raised their heads and pricked their ears. If she wasn't careful she would spook them.

"What's wrong?" Amy asked at his elbow.

Fargo pointed. "She was supposed to wait for us."

Amy took one look and burst from the shack, her arms and legs flying. Her dress hardly hindered her at all.

Catherine and Sarabell emerged. The moment Catherine saw Amy, she took off after her.

"Why is everybody in such a rush?" Sarabell whispered, Billybob once again straddling her hip. "Wouldn't it be safer to go slow?"

"There's a shortage of brains," Fargo said, and taking her arm, he started for the corral.

"I never did think very well. My ma used to say I was as dumb as a stump."

"I didn't mean you."

"Oh."

"Fact is," Fargo whispered, "you're the only one I can count on."

"Really?" Sarabell smiled and turned to Billybob. "You hear that, son? I'm doing something right for once."

Miranda had the gate wide but before she could go in Amy reached her and grabbed her and pulled her back. Miranda said something and pushed and Amy pushed back. Suddenly they were grappling and pulling hair.

Fargo ran.

Miranda was bigger and she was winning until Catherine grabbed her by the shoulders and slammed her to the ground. Both Catherine and Amy piled on, pinning her. So far they hadn't made much noise but Miranda made as if to shout just as Fargo reached them. Lunging, he clamped a hand over her mouth.

"Don't you dare, damn you."

Miranda bit him. She sank her teeth into the edge of his hand and locked her jaw.

Fargo tried to pull away and she clung tenaciously, drawing blood.

"What's she doing to you?" Catherine whispered.

Amy's arm moved. There was a *thuk* and Miranda went limp.

Amy dropped the rock she held.

"I'm obliged," Fargo said. His hand was throbbing. Moving past them, he approached the horses. Some were nervous but none whinnied.

Through them came the Ovaro. The stallion affectionately nuzzled Fargo's chest and he patted it.

"I'm glad to see you, too, boy." Fargo was especially glad that the rustlers had been too lazy to strip the saddle. He led the stallion out and went back into the corral for another.

"Hurry," Catherine urged.

Fargo chose the calmest animals. When he had enough he

closed the gate and turned. Amy and Catherine were already mounted.

"Should I climb on one too?" Sarabell asked. "I was waiting for you to say."

Fargo gave her a boost. He stood over Miranda, debating, and finally hooked his arms under her and slung her, belly down, over a bay.

"Just leave her," Catherine said.

"That's what she wanted to do with you." Fargo forked leather and reined around to leave.

A short distance off an outlaw sat up.

24

Fargo dropped his hand to his Colt.

The man gazed sleepily about, scratched himself, and sank back down.

"As quiet as you can," Fargo whispered to the women, and gigged the Ovaro, leading the horse that bore Miranda. Sarabell and Amy followed but Catherine's mount refused to move and she had to slap her legs to goad it.

The night was still. The wind had died and for a brief span the wild things were quiet.

Fargo rode at a walk until they had gone about a quarter of a mile. By then it was safe to ride faster. "We push on all night," he announced. None of the ladies objected. They were as aware as he was that their lives were in the balance.

It was about half an hour later that Miranda groaned and stirred and raised her head. "What's going on? Where am I?"

Fargo drew rein, reached over and grabbed her left leg, and dumped her to the ground.

"What in the hell?" Miranda came up as riled as a wet hen. She glared at everyone and focused on Fargo. "Now I remember. You hit me, you son of a bitch."

"No," Amy said. "I did."

Miranda took a step toward her.

"Don't even think it," Fargo said.

"Who's going to stop me? You?"

Fargo alighted and let the reins dangle. He turned, smiling, and punched Miranda in the gut. She tried to block it but he was too fast and too strong. Doubling over, she made choking sounds and gasped for breath. He took hold of the front of her dress.

Miranda growled and clawed at his face and he swatted her hand down.

"Do that again and I'll hurt you again," Fargo said. He hooked a foot behind her legs and pushed. Down she went, onto her backside. He waited until she stopped making sounds.

"Are you paying attention?"

"Go to hell."

"Twice now you've run out on us. We could have been killed because of you."

"I told you," Miranda said. "I look out for me. I don't give a good damn about the rest of you."

"It's sunk in," Fargo said. "So I want this to sink in, too." He bent down. "I've put up with all I'm going to. I told your father I'd get you to him but if you turn on us again, if you cause these women or me any trouble, any trouble at all, I'm taking your horse and we're going on without you."

"What kind of man are you? You'd strand a woman alone in the middle of nowhere?"

"Normally no," Fargo said. "But I'll be glad to make an exception with you."

"Bastard."

Sarabell kneed her horse up to them. "How can you be so mean?"

"The hayseed speaks."

"Stop calling her that," Fargo said.

"Sweet on her, are you?" Miranda taunted. She got her legs under her and stood, brushing at her dress. To Sarabell she said, "What you call mean I call smart. I don't owe you anything, sister. Neither you nor your brat."

Catherine said, "I've never met anyone so self-centered in my life."

"Me either," Amy said.

Miranda laughed. "Listen to all of you. Treating me like I'm the worst person alive when I'm doing what all of you want to do but don't have the gumption."

Fargo's disgust was boundless. Without another word he climbed on the Ovaro and resumed riding. Sarabell fell in beside him.

"I don't understand ladies like her."

"She's not," Fargo said.

"Not what?"

"A lady."

"But she's a colonel's daughter and all, and she wears nice clothes and talks good."

"You're more of a lady than she'll ever be."

"Thank you," Sarabell said. "It's right kind of you to say that."

"How's your boy holding up?"

"He's asleep right now."

"If your arm gets tired and you need to stop, say so," Fargo told her.

"You're awful nice to me," Sarabell said. "I'm not used to a man being nice."

Amy brought her horse up on the Ovaro's other side. "Do you have any idea where we're heading?"

"I do," Fargo said.

"Mind enlightening the rest of us?"

"Fort Lancaster is that way," Fargo said, and pointed in the direction they were going. "With any luck we'll run into

Colonel Crowley and his men long before we get there and you'll have an escort to the fort."

"And if we don't have any luck?"

"We do it on our own and it will be harder."

The next several hours were easy enough. No sign of pursuit developed.

Fargo called a halt to rest. Miranda brought her horse up to the Ovaro and stiffly dismounted.

"I'm so tired I can barely keep my eyes open. Can we sleep some?"

"No."

"Surely you don't intend to push on until you come across my father? That could take days."

"We're pushing on. You do what you want."

"You hate me, don't you?"

"I do," Amy said.

"Me as well," Catherine said.

Miranda put her hands on her hips. "I don't care what you bitches think. You haven't liked me since we met."

"Skye?" Sarabell said.

Fargo turned.

"What's that?" Sarabell asked, and nodded.

Fargo turned again.

A large bulk had reared dark against the stars.

25

"Don't anyone move or talk," Fargo said quietly. As big as it was, it could be one of two things: a bear or a buffalo. Since bears were more common in the hills and mountains and they were well out on the flatland, he suspected what it was even before it grunted and took several lumbering steps and pawed at the ground with a front hoof.

Sarabell and Amy and Catherine froze but Miranda turned toward it and blurted, "What the hell is that?"

The buffalo exploded into motion. It flew at Miranda but went past her and slammed into Catherine. She screamed as one of its curved horns hooked into her belly and ripped upward, lifting her off the ground. Without breaking stride the buffalo tossed her and pounded off into the darkness.

It happened so fast it was over before Fargo could draw the Colt. Even if he had, shooting it might have no effect. Buffalo were so massive that it took a large-caliber weapon to bring one down.

"Catherine!" Amy wailed, and was the first to reach her.

Fargo listened to the retreating drum of the buffalo's hooves. He figured it for an old bull. The old ones were often driven off by the younger, stronger bulls, and became loners, drifting where the wind took them until age or a pack of wolves brought them low.

Amy was on her knees, crying. Sarabell had a hand on her shoulder to comfort her.

Fargo went over. He had another gruesome sight to add to the many: Catherine on her back, blood seeping from her nose and mouth, her lips moving wordlessly, her body ripped open from her navel to her neck and her intestines in coils on and around her. Blood was everywhere.

"Oh God, oh God, oh God," Amy said between sobs.

"I'm so sorry," Sarabell said.

Miranda stood over Catherine. "She won't last long."

"I'm afraid not," Sarabell said sadly.

"Serves the bitch right for always giving me such a hard time."

Amy came off her knees in a burst of rage and tore into Miranda with her fists flying. She hit her several times and Miranda yelped and staggered back. Amy seized her by the hair and wrenched her to the ground and straddled her. She clamped her hands on Miranda's throat. Miranda rallied and punched Amy but Amy went on squeezing. Miranda bucked and raked her nails at Amy's face and still Amy's fingers gouged deep.

Sarabell glanced in shock at Fargo. "Aren't you going to do anything?"

In no great haste, Fargo took hold of Amy's arm and said, "Maybe you should stop."

"Maybe?" Sarabell said.

Amy's face was a mask of rage. She didn't seem to hear him.

Miranda's struggles were growing weaker. She flailed without energy and feebly kicked.

"You can't let her," Sarabell said.

"Oh, hell." Fargo wrapped his arm around Amy's waist and pulled. She clung on, fiercely determined to strangle Miranda no matter what. He wrapped his other arm and lifted and her body rose but her fingers were a vise. "Amy," he said in her ear. "You're killing her."

Amy gave a start. The wild gleam in her eyes slowly faded. Her body sagged and she raised her hands and looked at them as if she couldn't believe they were hers. "Oh God. What have I done?"

Fargo set her down.

"I almost did it," Amy said, staring aghast at Miranda. "I almost killed another human being."

"You were provoked."

"That's no excuse." Amy withered and pressed her hands to her face and sobbed.

Fargo didn't quite know what to say. He'd had to kill on occasion, nearly always in self-defense. He never lost sleep over it.

Sarabell put her free arm around Amy. "Don't be so hard on yourself."

"You saw," Amy said through her splayed fingers.

"Catherine was your friend," Sarabell said.

Amy bowed her head and closed her eyes. "That's no excuse. I should be able to control my temper."

"You need to sit a spell." Sarabell steered her away. "I'll keep you company."

Fargo squatted next to Miranda. She was taking deep breaths and her whole body quaked. She'd have marks on her neck for weeks. "That mouth of yours."

"I don't want to hear it."

"I pulled her off you this time but if there's a next time I won't."

"Go to hell, go to hell, go to hell."

Fargo went to the horses instead. He climbed on the Ovaro and leaned on the saddle horn, waiting. He hadn't said anything to the women but he wasn't all that confident Colonel

Crowley was still on his trail. It could well be they'd have to go all the way to the fort. The breeze shifted and he smelled a strong urine scent. From the wallow the buffalo had been lying in, he suspected.

Amy and Sarabell came up, Sarabell rocking Billybob on her hip.

"What are you doing up there?" Amy asked.

"We have a long way to go," Fargo said.

"Not without burying Catherine. We can't leave her for the scavengers. It wouldn't be right."

"What else can we do?"

"Bury her, of course."

"How?" Fargo said. "The ground is too hard to dig with our hands."

"Rocks, then," Amy said. "There have to be some around here somewhere."

"We leave her as she is. Say a few words over her if you have to and we'll be on our way."

"What kind of man are you that you can ride off and leave her like that?" Amy said. "That's harsh."

"So is life," Fargo said.

26

Fargo could practically feel their hatred. Amy hated Miranda and Miranda hated Amy. They constantly glared at one another. Neither would speak to the other. They were boiling pots on the verge of blowing their lids.

Sarabell was a breath of common sense. She didn't hate anyone. She stuck close to him during the day and at night she slept at an arm's length with Billybob tucked under the blanket in her arms.

By the second afternoon of their flight the women were weary from so much riding. Which was why, when Fargo came to the crest of a grassy bench, he drew rein and announced they would rest a while. He checked their back trail as he had done dozens of times—and his whole body tingled. In the distance were riders. That far off they were so many moving sticks.

Sarabell saw them too. "Is that the outlaws, you reckon?"

"Them or Comanches."

Amy raised a hand to her sweaty brow. "No matter who it is, we're in for it."

"I have a brainstorm," Miranda said. "Why don't we stake you out and leave you here? It might buy us time to get away."

"Go to hell, bitch."

"Please don't squabble again," Sarabell said.

"She's the one who has her head up her ass," Amy said.

"Is that a fact?" Fargo heard Miranda say, and damned if she didn't tuck her legs and spring from the top of her horse at Amy. Both pitched to the ground in a squall of curses and cries. Hitting and pulling hair, they tumbled back and forth. Amy was smaller but she was a hellion. Miranda fought dirty.

"Stop them!" Sarabell pleaded.

Fargo sighed. He was sick and tired of Miranda. For two bits he'd leave her. Swinging down, he tried to snag Miranda's arm but the women rolled out of reach. He grabbed at her leg and got a foot in his knee. The pain made him grit his teeth.

"Amy, look out!" Sarabell hollered.

Miranda had a rock. She was on top and had her other hand to Amy's throat. She raised the jagged-edged rock. If the blow landed it could kill Amy.

Fargo's hand leaped to the Colt and the revolver was out and the hammer back and he squeezed as smoothly as you please.

The boom of the shot and the burst of blood were simultaneous.

The rock went flying. So did Miranda's little finger. She shrieked and fell on her side and clutched her hand to her dress. "You shot me! You stinking bastard, you shot me!"

"You're still alive," Fargo said, and began to replace the spent cartridge.

Miranda hurtled up off the ground and swung at his throat.

Fargo sprang back and she missed but the blood spurting from her hand splattered his eyes and suddenly the world was a red blur. He wiped a sleeve across his face as a keg of black powder exploded between his legs. She had kicked him in the groin. He tried to stay on his feet but the pain was excruciating. As he fell to his knees she clubbed him on the ear. His vision cleared in time to see her scoop up the jagged rock and come at him again. He raised the Colt to shoot her but suddenly a horse filled his sights. Sarabell had ridden her animal into Miranda. Heaving upright, Fargo went around it.

Miranda was on the ground, swearing hotly, in the act of standing. Sarabell kicked her in the forehead. Then, out of nowhere, Amy appeared. She struck Miranda behind the ear with her closed fist and Miranda went limp.

"Damn," Fargo said.

"She sure is a tough one," Sarabell said.

"We should kill her while we can," Amy said. Snatching up the rock, she stood over Miranda.

"You can't," Sarabell said.

"Watch me."

"Go ahead," Fargo said. "If you don't mind it on your conscience."

"You're not going to stop me?"

"You feel you have to do it, do it," Fargo said. He honestly didn't care if she did or she didn't.

"Amy," Sarabell said.

"Hush."

"You need to hear me out," Sarabell said. She motioned at Miranda. "We have folks like her back to home. People who only ever think of themselves. People who lord it over others. I've never cottoned to them and I never will."

"Your point?" Amy said.

"My ma used to say that if we stoop to their level, we're no better than they are."

"I am better than her in every way."

"Not if you bash her brains out, you're not."

Amy looked at the rock in her hand and then at Miranda, and threw the rock into the grass. "Damn you, Sarabell. You should have let me." She turned and walked away.

"That would have been awful," Sarabell said.

Fargo was more interested in the riders. They weren't close enough to make out yet. Judging by the dust they were raising, there were a lot of them.

"We can't outrun them, can we?"

Fargo looked at her.

"I just don't want to die, is all."

"We think a lot alike." Fargo stepped to Miranda. Her hand was still bleeding but not badly. He slid the toothpick from its sheath and cut a strip from the hem of her dress and bandaged her. She'd have a stub where her little finger had been but she would live. Replacing the toothpick, he carried her to her horse and placed her on it, belly down.

"Shouldn't we wake her first?" Sarabell asked.

"You're a glutton for trouble," Fargo said.

An hour into the next stretch, Miranda came around. She didn't say a word. Fargo stopped and she slid off and stared at her bandaged hand as if trying to remember why it was bandaged. Then she climbed on her horse and sat there staring straight ahead.

"You all right?" Sarabell said.

Miranda didn't answer.

Fargo pushed on. By sunset they had put more miles behind them but they hadn't gained any. Their enemies stayed hard after them, and the dust cloud was twice the size it had been.

"Do you reckon they'll stop for the night?"

They were in the middle of a prairie with precious little cover. Fargo slowed to a walk and shifted in the saddle so he could watch the dust.

Amy hadn't spoken all afternoon but now she did. "I make it out of this alive, I'm heading back east and staying there. You can have the West."

"It's not all bad," Sarabell said.

"East of the Mississippi people don't attack wagon trains and kill most everybody and take the women."

"A few bad apples don't spoil the whole barrel."

"Will you just stop?" Amy said. "You always see the bright side in everything, even when there's no bright side to see."

Fargo rose in the stirrups. Was it his imagination, he asked himself, or had the dust cloud stopped? He stared and stared and finally smiled and said, "Ladies, we are in luck for once."

"We are overdue," Amy said.

In half a mile the prairie was broken by multiple washes. In the spring they were probably filled with water but now they were dry.

"We are in luck again," Fargo said, and descended a pebble-strewn incline and halted. "Someone gather brush and I'll get a fire going."

"Is that safe?" Amy said.

"It's not as if they don't know where we are." Fargo helped Sarabell down and turned to do the same with Miranda but she ignored his outstretched hand. "It won't hurt you to talk," he said.

Miranda held her hurt hand to her bosom and swung down. There were bloodstains on the bandage.

"After I turn you over to your father I think I'll stay drunk for a week," Fargo said.

Miranda put her good hand on the bandage. "Did you save it?"

"Save what?"

"My finger, you dolt. The one you shot off."

"Why in hell would you want that?"

"As a keepsake."

"You're not right between the ears," Fargo said. The gleam in her eyes bothered him. He left her and went up the incline and hunkered.

Pebbles clattered, and Sarabell was at his side. "Amy is collecting brush. What are you doing?"

"Getting the lay of the land straight in my head so after the sun goes down I won't get lost." Fargo was joshing. He never got lost.

"Surely you're not fixing to pay them a visit?"

"Surely I am," Fargo said.

27

Fargo needed to know. Were they outlaws? Were they Co-manches? He got a small fire going and about an hour after the sun went down stood and stretched and announced that he would be back before dawn.

The women had been quiet the whole time. Miranda wasn't talking anyway, but both Sarabell and Amy were not happy with his decision.

"I don't like you leaving us alone," Amy said. "We can't make it on our own."

"I'm not doing this because I want to," Fargo said. "I'm doing it because I have to."

"You should stick with us," Amy insisted.

"Maybe I can run off their horses," Fargo said.

"Maybe they'll kill you."

Fargo turned to the Ovaro and had his hand on the saddle horn when a hand touched his shoulder.

"Please be careful," Sarabell said.

"I always am."

Sarabell looked down at the ground and poked at the dirt with her toe. "I'm sort of fond of you."

"You're a fine lady," Fargo said.

She flashed him a shy smile. "You keep saying that. But I know I'm plain. I know I'm not all that smart. And I sure ain't refined like those rich ladies who sashay around in pretty dresses and ride in nice carriages."

"You have something a lot of them don't."

"What on earth would that be?"

"A heart." Fargo swung up and hooked his boot in the other stirrup. "I'm sorry I have to go."

"I understand why. I don't like it any better than Amy but I won't complain."

"Right there is what makes you fine," Fargo said. Bending, he leaned down and kissed her on the top of her head.

"What was that for?"

"Luck." Fargo raised the reins.

"You wouldn't happen to be looking to take a wife, would you?"

"No."

"You say that like you won't ever."

"Let me put it this way." Fargo smiled to lessen the sting. "There's no way in hell."

"Why not? I bet you'd make about the best husband there ever was."

Fargo laughed. "More likely the worst. The truth is, I like to wander more than I like anything."

"I know how men are," Sarabell said. "I know they can be restless, especially when they're young. But there comes a time when every man thinks about settling down."

"Maybe so," Fargo allowed. "But my time hasn't come yet." He gazed out over the expanse of night. "Ever since I can remember, I've had this urge to see what's over the next horizon. It's stronger than any urge I have. Even the urge to be with a woman. Any woman."

"Must be a powerful one."

"You do understand," Fargo said.

"Makes me sort of sad for you."

"Don't be. I like being how I am. I wouldn't have it any other way." Fargo glanced at the other two and lowered his voice. "Keep an eye on them. And whatever you do, don't let your guard down with Miranda."

"Oh, I wouldn't ever. She's not to be trusted," Sarabell agreed.

Fargo smiled and touched his hat brim and rode on up out of the wash. He had to admit that if he ever did give a thought to settling down, it would be with a woman like Sarabell. Maybe she wasn't a beauty. Maybe she wasn't elegant. But she had the quality he liked more than looks and schooling and manners.

The wind gusted, and the feel of it on his face brought Fargo out of himself. Here he was, thinking about romance, when he was running for his life with a pack of killers at his heels.

"I am damned silly."

He had a long ride ahead. He maintained a trot for a couple of miles and then went at a walk as much to spare the Ovaro as so the noise wouldn't carry and forewarn whoever was hunkered around the distant campfire.

The prairie was alive with the cries of coyotes. Once, from far off, came what Fargo thought might be the howl of a wolf but wolves were rare in those parts.

The fire grew in size to where he was sure no self-respecting Indian made it. Indians used small fires. White men made bonfires. So it wasn't Comanches.

It was shy of midnight when he drew rein within rifle range, and dismounted and stalked forward.

Most of them were asleep under their blankets. Rooster Tremaine, Luther Taft, the other Gonzales brother and a few others were still up. The horses were picketed in a string, and as Fargo watched, a sentry moved from one end to the other and started back again. Another man was walking the perimeter.

Fargo squatted. The way he saw it, he had two courses of action. He could shoot the leaders. With Rooster and Taft and the Gonzales brother dead, the rest might give up and go back. But he couldn't be sure he wouldn't only wound one or two, and that would make them only more determined. His other recourse was to run off their mounts. He began to circle.

The Gonzales brother got up and rubbed his belly and moved to his blankets. So did another man wearing a sombrero.

Rooster refilled his coffee cup. Taft was leaning back against his saddle with his arms folded.

Fargo moved with caution. The scrape of a boot or the snap of a twig would give him away. Whenever Taft raised his head in his direction, he stopped. He had made about half his circuit and had frozen for the tenth or eleventh time when something moved in the dark ahead. He thought it might be a deer or an antelope and stayed still so he wouldn't startle it. Then he realized that whatever it was, it was too low to the ground for either. It came toward him and was so close that he could hit it with a rock when the jolt of recognition was like a punch to his gut.

It wasn't an animal.

It was a Comanche.

28

The warrior was between Fargo and the camp, crawling with an agility a lizard would envy, his attention fixed on the outlaws.

Fargo scarcely breathed. His hand was on the Colt but he didn't want to use it. He kept expecting the Comanche to turn his head and see him but the warrior went on by and into the surrounding darkness.

Fargo flattened. Where there was one Comanche there were probably more. He knew how they worked. They had spotted the fire and come to investigate. Once they had a good idea of how many guns they were up against, they would decide whether to attack. If he continued to circle toward the horses, he ran the risk of running into them.

This changed everything. Fargo turned and crawled. He stopped often to look and listen. After he had gone more than a hundred yards and not seen any sign of the terrors of Texas, he considered it safe to rise and run. He had to get back to the women.

Fargo hoped the Comanches did attack. He hoped they wiped the outlaws out. Barring that, maybe the outlaws would turn back.

He half feared the Comanches had found the Ovaro but the stallion was where he had left it. Snagging the reins, he turned to climb on. The Ovaro lifted its head and gazed past him, and Fargo heard the whisper of rapidly padding moccasins.

He spun, streaking his hand to the Colt, just as a heavy body slammed into him. The impact knocked him against the stallion. Iron fingers clamped on his wrist. Colt steel swept at his neck. He barely got his hand up in time.

For an instant they were face-to-face, eye to eye. The Comanche hissed at being thwarted, and wrenched. Fargo was nearly flung off his feet. A leg hooked behind his and down he went with the warrior on top. The warrior put all his weight into trying to bury his knife. Fargo put all his strength into not letting him.

The Comanche was immensely strong. Inch by slow inch the tip came closer to Fargo's skin. He felt a prick and knew that in another few moments he would be bleeding like a stuck pig. In desperation he bucked and kicked and dislodged the man from his chest. Fargo rolled and drove his knee up and in and was rewarded with a grunt of pain. The Comanche hissed louder. With a mighty heave, the warrior tore free and went for Fargo's jugular. Twisting aside, Fargo shoved and pushed into a crouch. The Arkansas toothpick was in his hand before he stopped moving.

The Comanche raised his knife and threw himself at him, right into the rising arc of the toothpick. Fargo sank it to the hilt, and twisted. Again the warrior grunted, and gasped, and his powerful body melted like hot wax and he lay convulsing. In a minute it was over.

Fargo sat back, his arms over his knees, and hung his head. His whole body twitched, a nervous reaction to his close shave. He sat there until his arms and legs were still, and took a few deep breaths.

The Comanche's lifeless eyes were fixed on the stars. From under him spread a wet pool.

Fargo yanked the toothpick out and wiped the blade clean on the warrior's leggings. He slid it into the sheath and patted the Ovaro. "Thanks for the warning."

He got out of there. When he had gone far enough that neither the Comanches nor the outlaws would hear, he rode faster.

All the hard riding he and the women had done, the loss of sleep, had been for nothing. And now, with Comanches in the vicinity, they'd have to be twice as careful.

His instinct for direction served him well. He came to the wash almost at the very spot where he'd left it. One look, and he drew rein in consternation.

The fire had burned low. Only a few tiny flames flickered. They were enough to reveal a woman facedown with her arms outflung. Of the other two there was no sign. All the horses were gone.

Fargo swung his leg over and slid off and drew the Colt. Warily descending, he sank to a knee. The wound in the back of her head was hideous. The blow had shattered her skull and left a hole big enough to stick his finger into. He gripped her shoulder and rolled her over. To his surprise, her eyelids fluttered and opened. She had to try several times before she could speak.

"It was Miranda," Amy said.

"Figured as much."

"She snuck up behind me. I was sitting looking into the fire, and then there was the pain." Amy stopped and weakly licked her lips. "Sarabell tried to warn me. She yelled but I couldn't turn in time."

"What happened to Sarabell?"

"I don't know. When I came around they were gone. I tried to sit up but couldn't."

"When?" Fargo said.

"Not more than ten minutes after you left." Amy quaked and groaned. "I'm so cold. Like there's ice in my veins."

"I'll make the fire bigger," Fargo offered. It was the best he could do. They had no water left in his canteen, and no blankets.

"No," Amy said in a whisper. "I don't have long." She coughed and shuddered more violently and after a while she said, "Strange."

"What is?"

"I don't feel much pain where she hit me. Why should that be?"

"Did she say anything?"

"Yes." Amy's eyes were mirrors of fear. "Right after, she kicked me and I heard her laugh and say that I got what I had coming."

Fargo's own blood was on fire.

"Sarabell said something to Miranda and Miranda said that if Sarabell didn't mind her mouth, she'd be next."

Fargo looked up and down the wash.

"Miranda said she was going to finish me off. I think there was a scuffle. Then I blacked out." Amy sucked air into her lungs. "It's getting harder to breathe."

"Maybe you should stop talking."

"Your first name is Skye. Isn't that what you told us?"

"Yes."

"Do me a favor, Skye. Don't leave me lying here for the critters to chew on."

"I'll do what I can."

"Thank you." Amy managed a pale grin. "Life never works

out like you think it will." Suddenly she contorted in the worst spasm yet and when it was over she lay still with her neck at an angle and her tongue sticking from her mouth.

Fargo closed her eyes and opened her mouth and pushed her tongue back in, and stood. "It sure as hell doesn't."

29

Fargo spent half an hour covering Amy with rocks and dirt and brush. It was the best he could do. Next he went up and down the wash for a goodly ways. He came across no trace of Sarabell. He figured she had fled on horseback. And since he couldn't track at night without a torch, and if he used a torch the outlaws and the Comanches were bound to see it, he swallowed his worry and hunkered by the fire until the pink blush of impending dawn brightened the sky.

The tracks proved him right. Sarabell had run to her mount and galloped off to the west. Miranda had given chase.

Fargo vaulted onto the Ovaro and used his spurs. The women had four or five hours on him. A lot could have happened. In the dark it should have been easy for Sarabell to shake Miranda from her trail. Then again, Sarabell had been fleeing for her life and that of her child and might not have been thinking clearly.

The morning broke crisp. Life renewed its daily pageant. Black-tailed jackrabbits bounded off in high leaps. A sage hen took wing. A band of antelope were grazing to the south. A tarantula hawk wasp flew past his face, its red wings buzzing.

Ordinarily, Fargo would drink in the sights and sounds. Today he was riveted to the tracks. Sarabell had ridden over a mile at a gallop and finally slowed. Dogged after her came

Miranda. Soon the hoofprints showed where Sarabell goaded her animal to a gallop again. Maybe she had heard Miranda, Fargo reckoned. For another mile the chase was pell-mell. Sarabell's horse was likely growing winded by then and she slowed once more. So did Miranda. Their tracks paralleled one another off to the horizon.

Fargo swore. Miranda had no cause to kill Sarabell. Then he remembered that Sarabell hadn't let her take one of their horses back on the bluff. It would be just like Miranda to hold a grudge, and her grudges were the killing kind.

Fargo wondered how it was that a milquetoast like Colonel Crowley raised a murderous firebrand like Miranda. She had more sand in her shot-off little finger than he had in his whole body. But somewhere in her past she had gone bad.

Overhead, a sparrow hawk dipped and weaved. A gopher snake was searching for prey. From atop a small boulder a whiptail lizard watched him go by.

A tableland spread before him. Patches of zinnias splashed yellow here and there. A few filarees added spots of pink.

A burrowing owl rose from a prairie dog burrow.

Fargo rose in the stirrups, not really expecting to see anything, and a cold fist closed around his chest. A body lay sprawled amid the zinnias. Near it was a smaller form. "God, no," he said. The Ovaro flew. He was out of the saddle before it came to a stop and dropped to his knees and swallowed.

Sarabell was on her stomach, her hair over her face. Near her lay Billybob, curled in on himself.

Fargo placed a hand on her shoulder. "I'm sorry," he said softly.

"What for?" Sarabell sat up and threw her arms around him and pressed her face to his buckskins. "Oh, God, I'm happy to see you."

Fargo coughed. He saw that Billybob's eyes were open and the boy was sucking on his thumb.

"She took my horse and left us stranded," Sarabell said. "I thought we were goners."

"You're safe now," Fargo said huskily.

Sarabell pulled back. Tears trickled down her cheeks. "I heard your horse coming but didn't know it was you so I dropped down and played dead and told Billybob to lie still." She began to cry in earnest. "Amy is dead. I saw it with my own eyes. Miranda beaned her with a rock."

Fargo thought it best not to mention that Amy was alive when he found her.

"I tried to get away but she came after us. Followed me most of the night and snuck up when I stopped to rest. She's tricky, that one."

"Be glad she didn't try to bean you," Fargo said.

"She would have except I think she was too tired," Sarabell said. "She just took my horse and got on hers and headed for Santa Fe."

"You know that for a fact?"

Sarabell bobbed her chin. "Sure do. She came right out and told me. Said she wasn't going back to her pa. Not now or ever. It's why she wanted my horse. Santa Fe is a far piece."

That it was, Fargo reflected, across some of the most brutal terrain anywhere, terrain that was the haunt of the Apache. "She'll never make it."

"We have to go after her," Sarabell said, wiping her sleeve over her eyes.

"Like hell."

"You just said she won't make it on her own."

"Good riddance."

Sarabell put her hands on his arms. "You don't mean that."

"Like hell," Fargo said again.

Billybob took his thumb from his mouth and mewed like a kitten.

"What is it, sweetie?" Sarabell said, and plucked him to her bosom. "You remember Mr. Fargo, don't you?"

Fargo noted how tired she was. Exhausted was more like it. And no wonder. She'd hardly gotten any sleep the past two nights. "We'll rest here a spell and then go find those troopers from Fort Lancaster."

"What about Miranda?"

"Don't bring her up again." Fargo turned to the Ovaro and opened his saddlebags. The pemmican was still there. He held the bundle out to her. "Eat all you need."

Sarabell selected a piece and gave it to Billybob. "I can't not bring her up. We can save her if we hurry."

"My horse needs rest."

"Then after it has we go after her and bring her back whether she wants to come or not."

"Don't do this," Fargo said.

"I can't help being me," Sarabell said. "And it's not in me to let someone die if I can help it. Even if they deserve to."

"Damn you."

"I'm sorry," Sarabell said softly. "I couldn't live with myself and I don't believe you could either."

"You don't know me."

"I know enough."

Fargo gazed to the west. It was the biggest mistake they could make. He wanted to grab Sarabell and shake some sense into her. Instead he said, "We'll start after her at first light. For now let's find a spot to camp."

On the lee side of the mesa the slope had buckled. He descended into a fold where they were out of the wind and prying eyes wouldn't see their fire. There was no water and that was worrisome but Fargo didn't dwell on it. They ate more of his pemmican and sat and watched the western sky turn from azure blue to vivid orange and yellow and pink and then shade to gray and finally black. The stars were so many match tips. A soft breeze caressed the fold, and them.

The boy was soon asleep, bundled snug in one of Fargo's blankets, making soft snores.

Sarabell knelt beside him and put her hand on his brow. "He is all I have in this world."

"Yet you risk him for her," Fargo said.

"You're mad."

"I don't make a habit of fighting Apaches. They're too damn good at it."

"But you have," Sarabell said.

"Only when I've had to."

"We have to."

"If you were any more pigheaded you would have a snout," was Fargo's last volley.

Sarabell rose and came and stood in front of him, her navel near his nose, her body warm and her smile sad and yet happy. "You hate it when someone makes you be good. I feel the same sometimes." She put a hand on each side of his head and kissed him full on the mouth. The kiss was hunger and need and a lot more. When she broke the kiss she was breathless. "There's more where that came from if you're of a mind."

"No strings?" Fargo said.

"Nary a one. I've learned to enjoy what I can get and not fret over what I can't."

"If it helps any," Fargo said, and touched her cheek, "you are one of the few times I wished I was different."

"That's as high a compliment as I've ever gotten. I'm no beauty."

Fargo lowered his finger to her chest over her heart. "You are in here."

"Enough talk, then."

"More than enough," Fargo said.

30

Sarabell melted into Fargo. Her mouth was a furnace. Her hands were starved. She devoured him. He had been with a lot of ladies but few like her.

Her need fed his. Fargo grew so hard he thought he would burst his pants. Her caresses enflamed his ardor. Her fingers were always in motion, exploring, feeling. Every square inch of him felt her touch.

Of the many times Fargo had made love, most were blurs of memory. A few were as clear as the act. They were the special ones. The ones where the woman touched him inside. Sarabell touched him. It wasn't her looks or how she did the deed. It was her.

Their clothes wound up in a pile. Skin bare to the wind, Sarabell straddled him and gripped his member and grinned as she impaled herself. Inch by inch, until with a languid hump of her pelvis he was sheathed. She cooed and arched her back and her fingernails stung his shoulders. Her mouth met his mouth. Her breasts were perfect melons. He cupped and kneaded and pinched a nipple. She gasped and ground against him. He felt her moistness and the quivering of her walls.

Time drifted on currents of pleasure. Sensation piled on sensation until Fargo was on the brink. He refused to go over until she did. He nipped, he stroked, and he slid a hand between her thighs. Sarabell crested, her body a piston, her expression pure rapture. He matched her, surpassed her, lifted her with his thrusts.

In each other's arms they lay with the breeze now cool on their sweaty skin, and Sarabell ran a hand through his hair and kissed him on the chin.

"I'm obliged."

"Shouldn't the man thank the woman?"

"I'll remember you as long as I live."

"Maybe."

Sarabell nestled her cheek on his shoulder and closed her eyes. "No maybe about it. Just my luck you have the wanderlust." She snuggled and kissed him and said, "I think I'll sleep now."

Just like that, she was out. Fargo stroked her hair and smiled. He shifted to make himself comfortable and closed his own eyes. She wasn't the only one who had gone too long without sleep. He drifted off fully expecting to wake up in a few hours. But it was the heat of the sun on his face that brought him around. He blinked and blurted, "Son of a bitch."

Sarabell stirred and raised her head. "What's the matter?" she sleepily asked.

"It must be close to eight." Fargo eased from under her and commenced to dress. "We should have lit a shuck at daybreak."

"We needed the rest, I reckon."

Fargo had his pants on. He slipped into his shirt and sat and tugged his right boot on and then his left. He donned his hat and tied his bandanna around his neck and reached for the pearl-handled pistol he had taken from Gonzales.

"Leave your *pistola* where it is, senor."

Fargo whirled.

There were three of them. Their pistols were out and cocked. The tallest wore a sombrero and had a dazzling smile.

"We have been here a while. It was considerate of us, was it not, to let you sleep?"

Fargo looked past them.

"It is just us, senor. Gonzales and Tremaine sent us ahead. I am something of a tracker."

"Quit jabbering, Mendez, and let's tie him. Rooster won't like it if he was to get away."

Mendez sat on a boulder, his pistol pointed at Fargo. "He is not going anywhere, Tabor."

Sarabell had turned her back to them and was dressing as fast as she could.

"No need to do that, darling," Tabor said. "You're a pretty sight naked."

"She sure is," the third man agreed, and lecherously smacked his lips.

Mendez frowned and said to Fargo, "Where is it written a man cannot be a bandit *and* a gentleman?"

"What are you on about?" Tabor said. "I'm as much of a gent as you."

"You are a pig," Mendez said, "and Baxter there is more so."

Tabor colored and started to turn but Mendez shifted on the boulder and pointed his pistol at them.

"I would think twice, gringo."

"Damn your Mex hide," Tabor said.

"Careful," Baxter said. "Rooster doesn't like for us to pick fights with Gonzales's men."

"What if they do the picking?" Tabor angrily replied, but he kept his revolver trained on Fargo.

"I, too, am under orders not to provoke," Mendez said. "So why don't we pretend we like each other until the others get here?"

"Fine by me," Baxter said.

All the while they talked, Fargo was reaching for the pistol. He did it molasses-slow so they wouldn't notice. His hand was almost brushing the pearl grips when Mendez shifted back toward him.

"On your feet, gringo."

Fargo grabbed for the Colt.

31

Mendez fired but he shot at Fargo's hand to keep him from getting hold of the Colt, and missed. Fargo snatched it out and threw himself at the ground as Mendez fired a second shot that whizzed over his head. Fargo extended his arm and thumbed back the hammer and squeezed and Mendez's head snapped back as if he had been punched. The other two banged off shots and slugs kicked up dirt. Fargo shot Tabor square in the chest and then the third man. Tabor went to his knees but gamely raised his revolver. Fargo shot him in the neck. The third man was still on his feet and his next shot pinged off a rock inches from Fargo's face. Tabor was reeling but taking aim and Fargo put another slug into him. The third man turned to flee and Fargo emptied the Colt into his side.

In the sudden silence Fargo's ears rang. He glanced at Sarabell. She had Billybob pressed to her bosom and was hunched low, her back to the outlaws so she would take stray bullets and not the boy.

Fargo rose and went to Mendez. There was a hole between his eyes. Mendez had a Colt, too, and Fargo reloaded using Mendez's ammunition. As he inserted the last cartridge he moved to the others. Tabor was covered in blood and still breathing.

"You've shot me to ribbons, you bastard."

Fargo cocked the Colt and put the muzzle to Tabor's forehead. "I can shoot you again if you want."

Tabor coughed and blood gouted from his nose and the corners of his mouth. "Tate will get you. No one is better at killing than him."

"It's good to be good at something."

Tabor's gaze rose to the sky and his breathing became ragged. "It was stupid not to shoot you while you were sleeping," he said, and died.

The third man had already given up the ghost.

Fargo went through all their pockets and found twenty-three dollars and fourteen cents. He helped himself to Mendez's gun belt and strapped on the pearl-handled Colt. Their horses were hidden off a ways and he brought all three animals back. Two had canteens. In a saddlebag there was half a pound of jerky. "We are in hog heaven," he announced.

"Rooster and Gonzales will be awful mad," Sarabell remarked. "They'll want you dead worse than ever."

"They are welcome to try."

Sarabell stepped to a sorrel and rubbed its neck. "With all these horses we can outrun them, can't we?"

"Maybe. But once you're safe I have to go back."

She stopped rubbing. "Whatever for?"

"They have my revolver and my rifle."

"So? You have that other revolver now. Or you can take any of these others. And you can always get another rifle."

"You're right about the guns but I won't let them have them anyway."

"I don't understand. Is it because they are yours?"

"Yes."

Sarabell looked at him. "You are a prideful man—do you know that? But they are just guns. Your life counts for more."

Fargo shrugged.

"It's more than that, isn't it?" Sarabell said. "You don't like that they steal women."

"I'm glad they stole you," Fargo said, and winked.

Sarabell blushed.

"And they beat me and hung me from a tree and have tried to kill me," Fargo continued. "They have a lot to answer for."

"I see. You have your own code." She smiled. "You're a complicated man."

"I don't turn the other cheek, ever. Anyone hits me, I hit them. Anyone tries to kill me, I kill them. If that's complicated, then I am." Fargo didn't think it was.

"An eye for an eye and a tooth for a tooth," Sarabell said. "I can't read and I don't know much about the Bible but I remember that one."

"What do you live by?"

Sarabell kissed Billybob on the cheek. "I mainly just try to survive. Any day I'm breathing is a good one."

"Do you still insist on going after Miranda?"

"I do. We should catch her easy now, all the horses we have."

Fargo led the other two animals. They rode at a trot and changed mounts often so each was always fresh and that way covered twice the distance twice as fast. Toward noon Fargo spied something in the distance and drew rein. He pulled his hat low against the glare of the sun and stood as high in the stirrups as he could. "A horse."

Sarabell was squinting. "You can tell that from here? Goodness, you have good eyes."

"Must be one of hers."

"Why would she just leave it?"

"Let's find out."

It had been ridden near to exhaustion but that wasn't why. When Fargo gripped the reins and moved in a small circle, the horse limped. He examined its leg. "Damn her. She's ruined it."

"Won't it heal?"

Fargo shook his head and drew the pearl-handled Colt.

"Must you?"

"We can leave it and let it die slow. It'll take days and the horse will suffer every minute."

"No," Sarabell said. "I wouldn't want that."

Fargo had her take the horses on a short distance. He patted the stricken animal and put the muzzle to its head and said, "This should be her and not you." He stroked the trigger.

"You look mad again," Sarabell commented as he climbed on the Ovaro.

"I don't like to put down a horse when I shouldn't have had to."

"She only has the one left. We'll overtake her soon now, won't we?"

"By sundown."

"Promise me you won't shoot her on sight."

"No."

"You can't," Sarabell said. "You're not a cold-blooded killer."

"There are other ways," Fargo said.

32

The ground rose, broken and scarred by ancient upheavals. A line of tracks went up a boulder-strewn slope to a gap. Overhung by high walls of rocks, the gap was in perpetual shadow.

Fargo drew rein and rested his hands on the saddle horn. "Take a drink if you want."

Sarabell opened her canteen and raised it to Billybob's lips. After he swallowed a few times she took it away and took a single swallow herself. As she capped it she asked, "Something the matter?"

Fargo nodded at the gap. "Good spot for an ambush."

"She doesn't have a gun, does she?"

"Not that we know of." Fargo still didn't like it. His instincts warned him that something wasn't quite right and he had learned a long time ago that he ignored them at his peril. "Let me go first and stay back a ways."

"Be careful."

Fargo gigged the Ovaro and pulled on the lead rope. Hooves ringing on the rocks, he slowly climbed. He saw where Miranda had stopped partway up and turned her horse as if to check her back trail. Then she had gone on.

The gap was barely wide enough for a horse. Fargo stopped again about thirty feet below it. The shadow of the cliffs was darkest in the opening. He couldn't see what lay beyond.

Dismounting, he drew the Colt and climbed on foot. He

would make sure it was safe before he took the horses through. But he had taken only a couple of steps when there was a loud crash and the next instant a boulder the size of a watermelon came bouncing and sliding through the gap and straight at him. He flung himself aside and the boulder hurtled past. It missed the Ovaro but not the next horse. With a sharp crack it struck a front leg. The horse squealed and staggered and crashed to the ground as the boulder went skipping and sliding past Sarabell and Billybob and on down the slope another dozen yards before it came to a stop in a swirl of dust.

Fargo scrambled to his feet and ran to the Ovaro. As he grabbed the reins another boulder came hurtling out of the gap. Slightly smaller but no less deadly, it clattered and bounced and would have smashed into the Ovaro's head had Fargo not hauled on the reins. He pulled the Ovaro away from the opening. The third horse just stood there staring at the one that was down. He couldn't let go of the Ovaro to go to it so he yelled, "Here, fella, here!" but the animal didn't move. Bending, he grabbed a stone and threw it and the third horse broke into motion. He thought it would turn and run back down. Instead, it ran toward the gap.

Another boulder shot out. It hit the ground and arced up and smashed into the horse's head and felled it in its tracks.

Fargo went far enough to one side that the boulders couldn't harm them. Letting go of the reins, he sprinted for the opening. He was almost to it when he heard cold laughter and then another boulder bounded past. He stopped with his back to the cliff. It wouldn't be wise to enter the gap not knowing how far it went.

High-pitched tittering floated from the heights. Miranda was having fun.

Below, Sarabell gazed anxiously up at him.

Fargo inched to the opening and poked his head in. As

near as he could tell, the gap went about ten feet and then opened onto another boulder-covered slope. He ducked back.

"You still alive down there, handsome?" Miranda shouted, and did more tittering.

"I'm here, bitch."

"I heard a horse squeal. Did I get one?"

Fargo stared at the animal with the crushed skull and the other with the shattered leg, still kicking and trying to stand.

"You got two."

"You don't say?" Miranda said, and laughed. "Too bad I didn't get you or that hayseed."

"You can't keep rolling boulders down on us forever."

"Until dark will do," Miranda shouted. "Then I can slip away."

"Why'd you kill Amy?" Fargo hollered to keep her talking while he pondered his next move.

"Don't ask stupid questions," Miranda said. "You know damn well why. I hated the bitch and she hated me."

"You can't go around killing everyone you don't like."

"It's a shame we can't," Miranda said. "I'd have done in more than a few folks by now if it weren't that I couldn't stand being behind bars the rest of my life."

"You're loco," Fargo said.

"Don't tell me you haven't killed. I know better."

"Only when I have to."

"Same as me," Miranda said. "I had to kill that stupid cow. I couldn't take another minute of her treating me like I was dirt."

Fargo stuck his head into the gap again, trying to spot her. "What excuse do you have for leaving Sarabell and her boy to die?"

"She's nothing to me," Miranda answered. "She's lucky I didn't bash in her brains like I did the other one."

"The horse you took is dead," Fargo said to keep her talking. He had a fair idea where she was. "You ran it into the ground."

"It was a poor excuse for a mount. A stronger horse would have lasted longer."

"You don't have any regrets, do you?"

"Hell," Miranda said, and laughed. "I don't know the meaning of the word."

Fargo had pinpointed her voice as coming from behind a large boulder about forty feet up. To roll another down at him, she would have to come out from behind it.

"Cat got your tongue?"

"Make this easy for both of us," Fargo said. "Come out now with your hands in the air."

"And what? You'll take me to my father? I'd rather die."

"You're going one way or the other."

"Big words. Let's see you carry them out."

"Think I won't?" Fargo said, and charged into the gap.

33

Fargo ran full out. He saw Miranda pop from behind the boulder with a rock as big as a cannonball raised over her head. She hurled it down the slope and it bounced and skittered, gaining speed. He reached the end of the gap and threw himself to the left a heartbeat before the rock went crashing past.

Miranda cursed and disappeared.

Fargo went after her. Hooves drummed, and she reappeared on horseback. She lashed the reins and slapped her legs like a madwoman and the horse swiftly bore her up the slope and over the top of the mesa.

Fargo didn't stop. He didn't want her chucking more boulders. The slope was steep, the strain on his legs considerable. He reached the rim and burst on over but she was already out of pistol range and still using the reins and her legs.

Fargo didn't go back down until she was out of sight. Sarabell brightened and came to meet him. She stopped when he drew his Colt and pressed the muzzle to the stricken horse. At the blast the animal's legs stiffened and it nickered and was gone.

"I'm sorry you had to do that."

"It's another one I owe her," Fargo said.

"Did she get away?"

"Afraid so." Fargo replaced the spent cartridge and reclaimed the Ovaro. "Say the word and I can have you at Fort

Lancaster inside of a week. Or we might run into the colonel sooner."

"I'd like to push on."

"She's leading us into Apache country," Fargo thought it wise to mention.

"All the more reason."

"Two days, then."

"I beg your pardon?"

"I've gone along with you so far because I like you. But if we haven't caught up to her in two days, we're turning back." She went to speak and he held up his hand. "The Comanches are bad enough. The Apaches are worse. They live to kill. If you won't take that into account for your own hide, think of your boy."

"We can save her despite herself."

Fargo started toward the gap. "You're taking something for granted, Sarabell."

"What?"

"That I give a damn."

The mesa was arid, a prelude to the dry country that lay to the west. At that time of the year, with the sun an inferno, anyone foolhardy enough to try and cross it was baked alive.

Fargo tried to stay alert but the monotony of the heat and his fatigue combined to cause his eyelids to become as heavy as lead and his chin to dip. Each time he shook himself and jerked his head up but each time it was harder.

Sarabell had Billybob clasped tight. She took to dozing off too, and after the sixth or seventh time she cleared her throat and said, "I need a nap. Can we stop and rest a spell?"

There was no shade. She curled up in the shadow of her horse and within moments her bosom was rising and falling in regular rhythm. Fargo sat and ate jerky and watched a lizard skittle about. The only other living creature in all that sea of blistering heat was a lone buzzard circling in search of carrion.

The sun was on the horizon when they made camp in scrub oak. Fargo stripped the horses and cleared a space for their fire. Where there was vegetation there was usually wildlife and he hadn't gone far when he spooked a rabbit that made the mistake of stopping to look back to see if he was giving chase. He skinned it and cut the meat into chunks and added a few wild onions he had found, and water, and brought it to a boil. A simple stew, yet after days without a meal, it was downright delicious. He gorged on three helpings. Sarabell had four. When they were done they both laid back and patted their bellies and Sarabell groaned.

"I hurt, I ate so much. But it's a good hurt."

Billybob was so tired he was asleep shortly after the sun went down. Sarabell tucked him in and came over to the fire and sat so she faced Fargo.

"Can you guess what I'd like for dessert?"

Fargo laughed and pulled her to him. "A woman after my own heart."

Their coupling was fierce and passionate, and afterward she lay on his chest entwining her fingers in his hair and looking happy and content. They fell asleep that way.

Fargo opened his eyes with a start. The chill of the night on his bare skin had awoken him. He slid from under her and dressed, then covered her and added broken branches to the fire.

The food and the sleep had done wonders. He felt invigorated.

Around him the night was uncommonly still. Even the coyotes were silent.

In that awful quiet a shrill cry was borne on the wind from

out of the west. A human cry of fear and pain. It was abruptly cut off.

Fargo listened but it wasn't repeated. He didn't mention it to Sarabell when she rose at the crack of the new day. But it was much on his mind as he led her out of the oaks and off across barren land where death ruled with a heavy hand. They passed the bleached bones of a deer and later the withered remains of a partially eaten raccoon.

From atop a knoll they could see for miles. They saw the horse as clear as anything but not the holes in its sides and neck until they drew rein. Flies buzzed and crawled in their hundreds.

"Arrows did that?" Sarabell asked, holding Billybob to her bosom.

Fargo nodded.

"Why didn't they leave them sticking in? And why kill a horse, anyway? Didn't they need it?"

"Apaches can cover as much ground on foot as whites can on horseback," Fargo enlightened her. "And arrows take a lot of time and effort to make so they don't leave them behind."

"You're sure it was Apaches?"

Fargo pointed at tracks. "Those were made by Apache moccasins."

"But where's Miranda?"

They walked on, Fargo seeking right and left for sign. He spied two red lines, and stopped. The lines were broken into tiny particles and each particle moved. They were red ants.

"Maybe you should stay here."

"With Apaches around?"

The red line wound among rocks slabs and boulders to a clear spot. Miranda Crowley, as naked as the day she came

143

into the world, was spread-eagle, her wrists and ankles secured to stakes.

Sarabell took one look and turned quickly away and doubled over. "Oh, God. I think I'm going to be sick."

Fargo didn't blame her.

Miranda had been skinned alive. Her fingers and toes lay in piles at the end of each limb. A strip of hair had been cut from the middle of her head. Without her skin her body was a hideous grotesquery, her exposed flesh and the blood a beacon for the red ants and a horde of flies. The ants were tearing at her with their sharp mandibles and carrying bits and pieces back to their nest.

Fargo went closer. Her chest was rising and falling; she was alive. Her eyes had been slashed, her nose split. She must have heard him because she licked her parched lips.

"Who's there? More of you red filth?"

"It's me," Fargo said. As an afterthought he said, "And Sarabell."

"You must be enjoying this."

"No."

"I spit on them," Miranda said proudly.

"You what?"

"They tore off my clothes and were pushing me back and forth and I spit on one of them. Spit right in his eye." She croaked a harsh laugh.

"So they cut yours," Fargo said.

Miranda's smirk faded. "I hurt so much for a while there. I screamed and screamed. But now it's not so bad."

Fargo saw a red ant peel a sliver of flesh. "Would you like some water?"

Miranda didn't answer right away. When she did he could barely hear her. "Get it over with."

"You shouldn't have gone off on your own," Fargo said

as he drew the pearl-handled Colt and thumbed back the hammer.

"All I wanted was to be my own woman. I didn't deserve this."

Fargo thought of Amy with her skull caved in and Catherine with her intestines ripped out and the farmer Miranda had married so she could get away from her father, slaughtered by Rooster Tremaine's men. "Yes," he said, "you did."

He shot her.

34

The troopers had camped near a spring. Everything was in military order. Tents were up, the horses were picketed, sentries had been posted. One of them challenged Fargo and Fargo glared at him and he lowered his rifle.

Soldiers quickly converged, Corporal Brunk towering over the rest. Colonel Crowley and Major Hargrove came out of a tent, Crowley buttoning his jacket over his rotund bulk.

"There you are!" Crowley said. "Your arrival is most timely. We lost your trail. I was about ready to turn back." He peered up at Sarabell and Billyboy. "That's not my daughter. Where is she? Who are they?"

Fargo dismounted. He walked around the Ovaro and gave Sarabell a hand down and turned to Captain Baker. "Would you see that they're fed and find a tent they can rest in?"

The young officer nodded and smiled. "This way, ma'am, if you please."

Crowley grew red in the face. "I give the orders around here. Now answer my question. Who are they? And where's my daughter? You went off to rescue her, not this ragamuffin."

Any shred of sympathy Fargo had for the man evaporated. He gave it to him straight. "Miranda is dead."

The colonel winced as if he had been stabbed. "I knew I shouldn't get my hopes up. How? Who? Where?"

"Apaches."

"Apaches?" Crowley repeated. "I thought you were certain she was abducted by white men pretending to be Comanches? How in blazes do Apaches enter into this?"

"Coffee," Fargo said. He was weary from his ordeal. They had pushed hard to get here with one eye always on their back trail. "And food."

Major Hargrove stepped forward. "Now see here—"

"No," Colonel Crowley said, with a wave of his hand. "Look at his clothes. Look at his face. This man has been through hell. I've waited this long. I can wait a few minutes more."

Fargo sat at a fire and ate a plate of beans and drank coffee, and told them. Everyone except the sentries listened with rapt attention. He told them everything, more or less. When he got to the part where Miranda had run out on him at the rustler's hideout, he glanced at the colonel and didn't mention it. He didn't mention how her blunder got Catherine killed by the buffalo, or that Miranda had murdered Amy.

"So her strong-willed nature got her killed," Crowley said sadly when Fargo finished. "If she hadn't of run off on you, the Apaches wouldn't have gotten her." He sucked in a breath and bowed his head. "Well, I guess we're done, then. We can head back to the fort."

"What about the women-stealers?" Fargo said. "Rooster Tremaine and his bunch."

"They could be anywhere by now. How would we find them?"

"I could."

"There are how many of them? Twenty, you said? All of them well armed." Crowley shook his head. "No, I won't risk my command."

147

"You have twice as many men."

"What would be the point?" Crowley said. "All the women are dead except the one you brought in."

"Someone has to stop them or they'll do it again and go on doing it from now until hell freezes over."

An unlikely ally cleared his throat. "I agree with Fargo, sir," Major Hargrove said. "These scum must be punished. After all, they stole your daughter. Indirectly they are to blame for her death as much as the Apache."

"I have made my decision," Crowley said testily.

"Very well," Hargrove said. "But I will put in my report that I protested in the most vigorous terms. If we don't stop them, who will? Fargo is right. They'll go on stealing women for as long as they can."

"Damn it, man."

Fargo drained his cup and set it down. "Why don't you try being one for a change?"

"Eh?" Crowley said. "Be what?"

"A man."

"Now see here."

Fargo rose until he towered over the colonel and poked him in the chest, hard. "Your own daughter was taken. They would have raped her if I hadn't come along. Now she and those others are dead, and you want to ride back to the fort and sit on your fat ass and do nothing?"

"Don't talk to me like that."

"Look around you," Fargo said.

"What?"

"Look at your men."

Nearly every face mirrored disgust if not outright loathing. Crowley blanched, and coughed, and shifted his weight from one foot to the other. "They don't understand. Command weighs heavy on my shoulders. I must do what is best for everyone, not just for me."

"For once in your life," Fargo said, "don't be yellow."

"I won't stand here and be insulted." The colonel wheeled and barked, "Out of my way." But none of the men moved. "What is this? Didn't you hear me?"

Hargrove stepped in front of him. "You need to give this more thought, sir."

"Enough, Major."

"The army doesn't like to be embarrassed, sir, and it will be when the newspapers get hold of the story."

"The newspapers?"

"Yes, sir. The attack on the wagons. The kidnapped women. It will be all over the country. As will the fact that you didn't go after those responsible."

"I forbid you or anyone else here from talking to journalists."

"You can't forbid me," Fargo said.

Crowley had the aspect of a cornered animal. His eyes flicked from side to side as if he sought to escape. "Damn you, anyhow. You have me backed in a corner."

"Then we'll go after them, sir?" Major Hargrove asked.

"You will," Colonel Crowley said. "I'll escort the young lady to the fort. Take thirty of the men. The remaining ten will go with me."

"Whatever you say, sir."

Crowley motioned and this time the men parted and he scurried to his tent.

"God," Major Hargrove said.

"I'm going with you," Fargo said.

Hargrove turned. "Glad to have you. I know you don't like me and I don't particularly like you, but in this we agree. Those sons of bitches must be punished."

"You figure to take them alive and bring them back to stand trial?"

"Hell no. I intend to wipe them out to the last goddamned man."

Fargo smiled. "Then we do agree."

35

As they prepared to head out at first light the next morning, a hand fell on Fargo's arm.

"You wouldn't go without saying good-bye, would you?" Sarabell said, sounding hurt that he hadn't.

Fargo hugged her and she kissed him on the cheek. Behind her, Captain Baker held Billybob.

"I can't ever thank you proper for what you've done. Words just aren't enough."

"I hope you have a good life," Fargo said, and meant it.

"I have an aunt who was always fond of me. I'll get word to her. Maybe she'll be willing to put us up until I figure out what I want to do with my life." She glanced over her shoulder at Baker, who had commenced to bounce Billybob on his arm and make coo-coo sounds. "Or maybe I'll hang around the fort a while and see what develops."

"You'll do fine."

"How can you be so sure?"

"Tremaine, Luis, the rustlers, Apache country, you've survived them all," Fargo said. "You're a tough little lady."

Sarabell smiled and touched his chin. "I won't forget you," she said softly, and then she wheeled, took her son from the captain, and walked hurriedly away.

"Don't worry," Baker said. "I'll make sure she gets to the post safe."

"She's a good woman. She deserves a man who will treat her right."

Baker grew thoughtful, nodded, and went after her.

Major Hargrove and the thirty troopers under him were already mounted and waiting. "Whenever you're ready," Hargrove said.

Fargo stepped into the stirrups.

Hargrove pumped his arm and bawled a command and the column headed out.

Fargo hadn't gone ten feet when the Ovaro acquired a giant shadow on a bay.

"Remember me?" Corporal Brunk said.

"What do you want?"

"Hey, now," Brunk said, and grinned. "I'm trying to be friendly here. The major says I'm to stick by your side like the captain did."

"Wonderful," Fargo said.

"What harm can it do, me covering your back?" Brunk said. "Fact is, I've come to respect you."

"Lucky me."

"I'm serious," the big soldier said. "There aren't many I'll say that about. I'll try to get along if you will."

The corporal was true to his word. He was a mean drunk but he was a good soldier and he gave Fargo no cause to be annoyed at him.

Hargrove, on the other hand, annoyed Fargo no end. He was too brusque with his men. He was proud of his rank, and woe to the man who didn't do exactly as he was told. To his credit, Fargo noticed that Hargrove stressed safety above all else. Point and flank riders were always out during the day, and always in pairs. At night twice the usual number of sentries patrolled the perimeter. Fargo still didn't warm to him, though, until the evening of the fourth day. Hargrove finished his supper and rose and raised his arms.

"Your attention, men. The scout tells me that tomorrow we'll reach the rustlers' camp. It could be that the women-stealers, Rooster Tremaine and his men, are still there. Either way we'll have a fight on ours hands."

"I can't wait," Brunk said.

"I want each of you to look to your weapons. Make sure that your carbines and revolvers are cleaned and loaded. When we engage the enemy, no one is to do anything rash. No one is to play the hero. I don't want to lose a single man. Is that understood?" A lot of heads bobbed. "Good. Follow my orders implicitly and we can get through this together."

It was the middle of the next afternoon when Fargo and Hargrove and Brunk crept to the edge of the bluff overlooking the corral. Hargrove swept the cabins and shacks with his binoculars.

"I only count nine."

"Might be a few more inside," Corporal Brunk said.

"Rooster Tremaine and his men aren't here, damn it." Fargo had hoped to end it. "Those are just the rustlers."

"The less of them, the better for us." Hargrove twisted toward Brunk. "Corporal, you'll take half the men and form a skirmish line a hundred yards to the east of the camp. I'll do the same to the west. When you hear the bugler, we'll charge from both sides and catch them between us."

"Do we take any alive, sir?"

"We do not."

"Hold on," Fargo said. "They might know where Tremaine went."

Hargrove considered that, and nodded. "Very well. I amend my order, Corporal. Try to take one or two alive if you can."

"Yes, sir."

Fargo stayed on the bluff. He didn't think the rustlers would offer much resistance but they surprised him. As the metallic notes of the bugle rent the air, they scrambled for cover. The surviving Gonzales brother came out of the cabin his brother had died in, strapping on a pistol. From a shack ran others. A ragged volley was fired at the advancing troopers but only two soldiers fell, and then the rest were on the rustlers in a blur of bloodshed. Carbines cracked, revolvers boomed, men screamed and men died. Corporal Brunk rode down a fleeing rustler and crushed the man's head, sombrero and all, with a sweep of his carbine's stock. Major Hargrove shot another in the face. Several rustlers got the corral gate open and tried to flee and were picked off in the act of mounting.

It was over quickly. Bodies littered the earth. Only one other trooper fell, from a shoulder wound.

When Fargo rode up, three rustlers were still breathing. They had been brought to the corral. One had lead in his belly. Another had a bullet hole in his leg. The last was unhurt and sat with his chin thrust defiantly.

"You wanted to talk to a few and here they are," Major Hargrove said. "Don't say I never did you a favor."

Fargo swung down and stepped up to the man who was unhurt.

"Where did Rooster Tremaine get to?"

"Go to hell, gringo."

Fargo slowly drew the Colt and slowly cocked it and slowly pointed it at the man's boot. "I didn't hear where."

"I will die before I tell you."

"Maybe not," Fargo said, and shot him in the foot. The man howled and grabbed his leg and flopped wildly about. Fargo waited until he was still and said, "One more time. Where's Rooster?"

"It won't do you any good. He has too much of a start."

"Let me be the judge," Fargo replied, and shot him in the other foot. The thrashing took longer and ended with the rustler limp and dripping with sweat. "Third time," Fargo said. "Or I put one in your middle leg."

"My middle—?" The rustler tried to back away and bumped a rail.

Fargo cocked the Colt.

"All right! All right! I'll tell you! Tremaine is on his way to Mexico. He left here two nights ago."

Fargo let down the hammer and half turned. "My rifle and my revolver?"

The rustler was gritting his teeth and groaning but he stopped to say, "Luther Taft took your Henry. He likes how shiny it is. I don't know about the other."

Fargo went from body to body but none had his Colt. He checked the buildings, too. As he emerged from the last shack three shots rang out.

The wounded troopers were left under the care of three others. The rest mounted and the column re-formed. Major Hargrove was all smiles when Fargo brought the Ovaro up.

"What are you so happy about?"

"I just love the smell of gun smoke and blood."

"There will be a lot more of it before we're through," Fargo predicted.

36

Twenty riders left a lot of tracks and they all pointed to the south, toward the border.

Major Hargrove was determined to catch them before they reached it. "Once they cross over, we're licked. My superiors would have my head on a platter if I crossed into Mexico."

"We have two days to make up," Fargo reminded him.

"And we will."

They rode all of that day and on through the night, stopping only briefly for snatches of rest. After five hours of sleep they were in the saddle again. Cavalry mounts were accustomed to long patrols under harsh conditions but this tested their stamina.

It tested the Ovaro's, too. Every time they stopped Fargo filled his hat and let the stallion drink. By that evening he was feeling the effects himself.

Shortly after the evening meal, as everyone sat around relaxing, a sentry ran up to Major Hargrove.

"Sir! You need to come see this."

Several miles to the south an orange glow writhed as if alive.

"Is it them, you think?" Corporal Brunk wondered.

"Who else would it be?" Major Hargrove said.

"Comanches, maybe," Fargo replied, although he was inclined to doubt it.

"I'll send a man ahead to see," Hargrove proposed. "Corporal, smother our fire. I don't want them to know we're here."

"Yes, sir."

"I should be the one to go," Fargo said.

"Why you?"

"I've lived with Apaches and some of their sneakiness rubbed off."

Hargrove snorted. "That's not the real reason. Go ahead if you want. But I want your word you won't start anything without me and my men there."

"What could I do by myself?" Fargo said, and went about saddling the Ovaro. He wasn't in any rush. Tremaine wasn't going anywhere. As he rode past Hargrove he said, "Have your men keep their hardware handy."

"Remember what I said."

The night was black as tar. There was no moon and scattered clouds blocked much of the starlight.

Fargo rode slowly. He would like for most of Tremaine's cutthroats to be under their blankets when he got there.

As it turned out, besides a guard by the horses, only Tremaine and Luther Tate and one other man were still at the fire, talking.

A bright gleam in Tate's lap made Fargo clench his jaw muscles. He was close enough to hear but not close enough for them to make out his silhouette against the sky.

"We'll be at the Blazedale ranch in three days," Tremaine was saying. "From there it's only another day to the border."

"Do you think his daughters are as pretty as everyone says?" Tate asked.

"We'll find out. They should fetch a good price from Hernandez." Tremaine drank the last of his cup and set it aside. "Too bad about those other women. That colonel's daughter would have brought twice as much as most."

"She was only fair-looking," Tate said.

"It was who she was, not her looks. A lot of our kind don't care for the army."

"I'm one of them."

"Think of how much some would pay for the privilege of beating an officer's daughter."

"Or for the chance to poke her," Tate said.

Tremaine grinned. "That too." His grin died. "Whoever that hombre in buckskins was, he cost us a lot of money. Three women dead and the other one got away."

"You should have let me go after him."

"I need you here with me."

Fargo drew the pearl-handled Colt and cocked it. He didn't have long to wait before Tremaine stood and stretched. Fargo gigged the Ovaro. Tate had followed suit, the Henry in the crook of his arm. They were moving toward their blankets and had their backs to him. The man at the fire was half dozing. Fargo jabbed his spurs. They heard him, of course, and spun, but by then he was into the firelight and he pointed the Colt and shot Rooster Tremaine in the forehead. Luther Tate started to level the Henry and Fargo shot him in the face, and as Tate began to fold, Fargo shoved the Colt into his holster and swung low and ripped the Henry from Tate's hands. In another moment he was up and out of the light. Behind him yells rose and curses were punctuated by the blasts of guns.

Fargo reined around and stopped. He ran his hand over the Henry and jacked the lever to feed a cartridge into the chamber.

The women-stealers were milling about in confusion. Only one man had run to the horses and he was standing there bellowing for the rest to mount up.

Again Fargo pricked his spurs. He wedged the Henry to

his shoulder and as he burst in among them he fired at face after face after face, working the lever as fast as he could work it. Twisting right, he fired. Twisting left, he fired. The Henry held fifteen shots and he emptied the magazine and was off into the dark again with hornets buzzing about his head.

Fifty feet out Fargo drew rein. How many were down was hard to say. Others were rushing to their mounts. He shoved the Henry into the saddle scabbard and was about to haul on the reins and get out of there when the bugle pealed and out of the night swept the U.S. cavalry. They flashed past on either side, their accoutrements clattering, their weapons at the ready.

At a bawl from Hargrove a volley tore into the outlaws, both those who were on their feet and those who were down. Not a man was spared. They were pierced and shredded. It was a bloodbath.

The troopers charged clear through the camp, wheeled in tight order, and charged again. Any outlaw who moved, any body that twitched, became a sieve.

Once more the troopers wheeled. Major Hargrove barked another command and they slowed and entered the camp at a walk. Corporal Brunk and others climbed down and went from still form to still form, making sure. One of the outlaws sat up and reached out with a bloody hand and asked for help. Brunk blew his brains out.

Fargo rode over.

"Well, well, well," Major Hargrove said.

"I thought you were going to wait for me to get back," Fargo said.

"I was," Hargrove replied. "Until I got to thinking about how you didn't give me your word you wouldn't do anything on your own."

"I owed them."

"It was a damn fool stunt and it could have gotten you killed."

Fargo climbed down. He went from body to body checking holsters and scouring the grass but on his first pass he didn't find it. He started rolling the bodies over. The seventh one, there his Colt was, under the dead man. He picked it up and twirled it, and smiled. Sliding the pearl-handled Colt out, he let it drop and slid his own into his holster.

Hargrove and Brunk had been watching.

"You went to all that trouble for a revolver?" the major said.

"I'm used to it." Fargo climbed on the Ovaro. "I take it you can find your way back to the fort without my help?"

"I think we can manage," Major Hargrove said. "Where are you off to?"

"Anywhere but here," Skye Fargo said, and turned his face into the wind.

LOOKING FORWARD!
The following is the opening section of the next novel in the exciting *Trailsman* series from Signet:

TRAILSMAN #353
BITTERROOT BULLETS

The mountains of western Montana, 1861—where only the brave dare venture, and few who do ever come out again.

The trading post was on a stream that fed into the Mussel-shell River. Skye Fargo had been there before. In addition to supplies, the owner sold whiskey, and Fargo was hankering for a bottle of red-eye. He thumped the counter and paid and took a corner table, as was his habit, with his back to the wall.

At another table four men were playing cards. Three wore buckskins, like Fargo. Unlike him, they didn't have his habit of bathing now and then and they stunk to high heaven of hides and guts and sweat. The fourth man wore a suit and a bowler.

Besides the owner there was a kid sweeping the floor. The kid kept glancing at Fargo.

A big man, broad at the shoulder and lean at the hips, Fargo was used to being stared at. He had a Colt on his hip and a splash of vanity at his throat in the form of a red bandanna. As he opened the bottle and poured, he heard an oath from the other table and one of the hide hunters smacked his dirty hand down.

"That's the third in a row, you son of a bitch. You better not be cheating."

The man in the bowler raked in his winnings, saying, "I don't need to cheat, friend. They don't call me Lucky Ed for nothing."

Fargo opened the Monongahela and filled his glass to the brim. He sniffed it, smiled, and emptied the glass in a swallow, then sat back as the liquor warmed him all over. He was tipping the bottle again when two women came out of the back. Right away his interest perked.

One was older than the other by a considerable number of years but both were easy on the eyes. The oldest had black hair, the youngest was a redhead. Their dresses swelled nicely at their bosoms and hips. Their ruby lips were spread in warm smiles.

"Well, now," said the oldest, who had to be in her thirties, as she stopped at Fargo's table. "What do we have here?"

"He's awful handsome," the youngest said. She looked to be all of eighteen, if that.

"Ladies," Fargo said, and devoured them with his eyes. "Why don't you join me?"

"Don't mind if we do," said the oldest. She winked at the young one and they pulled out chairs. "I'm Brianna. This here is Calypso."

"Calypso?" Fargo said. It was a new one to him.

"My ma got it out of a book," Calypso said. "She thought it had a pretty sound."

Fargo raised an arm and caught the owner's attention and pointed at the women. The owner nodded and promptly brought over two more glasses.

"Don't forget we have other customers," he said to the women as he set the glasses down.

Brianna glanced over her shoulder and frowned. "I'd rather not, Tom. They get awful rough."

"It's your job," Tom said.

"Not to be beat, it ain't," Brianna said.

"The last time all Kroenig did was slap you," Tom persisted.

"Six times." Brianna held her ground. "My cheek was swollen for a week."

"I'll protect you," Tom said.

"That's what you said last time."

"Damn it, Bri—"

Fargo looked at him and drummed his fingers on the table. Tom noticed, and swallowed heavily.

"Sorry. We shouldn't squabble in front of you, should we?"

"Well now," Brianna said as Tom walked off, "that was interesting. All you did was stare at him and he tucked tail."

"Tom knows me," Fargo said. He filled their glasses and took a sip from his own.

Brianna placed her elbows on the table and her chin in her hands and studied him. "Tom Carson ain't a kitten. What makes you so special that he treats you with so much respect? You don't look mean so it must be something else."

"You look handsome," Calypso made a point of saying again.

To change the subject Fargo asked, "You ladies worked here long?"

"Going on a couple of months," Brianna replied.

"You don't sound happy about it."

"We're not. There's not enough trade to keep us busy. I am bored half the time and there's nothing I hate worse in this world than being bored."

"I hate runny noses," Calypso said.

Brianna had more to complain about. "When Tom hired us he made it sound better here than it is. Claimed we'd make a hundred dollars a month, easy. Hell, we're lucky if we make half that much."

"Why do you stay?"

"We agreed to stick for half a year and I'm a woman of my word."

"Nice body, too."

Brianna chuckled and reached across and put her hand on his. "I am commencing to like you. Do you plan to stay the night?"

"If he is we should flip a coin," Calypso said. "I like him too."

"What about them?" Fargo said with a nod at the other table.

"They can play with themselves for all I care."

Brianna said it too loudly. All three buffalo men shifted in their chairs and the largest got up and came over.

"Were you talkin' about us, whore?"

"Leave me be, Kroenig," Brianna said.

"I don't believe I will," Kroenig declared, and grabbed her arm.

No other series packs this much heat!

THE TRAILSMAN

National Bestselling Author

RALPH COMPTON

GRITTY WESTERN ACTION FROM
USA Today BESTSELLING AUTHOR

RALPH
COTTON

Available wherever books are sold or at
penguin.com

S909-0930

Charles G. West

**"RARELY HAS AN AUTHOR PAINTED THE
GREAT AMERICAN WEST IN STROKES SO
BOLD, VIVID AND TRUE."
—RALPH COMPTON**

The Blackfoot Trail

Mountain man Joe Fox reluctantly led a group of
settlers through the Rockies—and inadvertently into
the clutches of Max Starbeau. Max had traveled with
the party until he was able to commit theft and
murder—and kidnap Joe's girl.

Also Available
Ride the High Range
War Cry
Storm in Paradise Valley
Shoot-out at Broken Bow
Lawless Prairie

Available wherever books are sold or at
penguin.com

S805-111510